What People Are S~~aying~~  *~~Da~~mascus*

There is a rhythm to this s~~tory~~ ~~in yo~~ur head.
A relaxing melody that ma~~kes you happy. The story uses~~ Islam as the central philosophy of the journey of a man who prepares the world for the second coming of Christ. Yet, this is not a story of religion. It is a look at morality - and the impact of choices not only on those who make them, but the ripple effect of those choices through society.
★★★★ Palla O'Neal-Jimentel, Parkville, MD

Omar Imady's The Gospel of Damascus attempts to eradicate this severance between mankind and helps to unite Muslims, Jews, and Christians by connecting the three belief systems together. The author shows tremendous respect for all three religions, and I very much appreciated how he was able to use factual aspects of the three different religions and incorporate them into a fictional story. The Gospel of Damascus was an absolute pleasure to read!
★★★★½ Jason Roberts, Cambridge, Ontario, Canada

I thoroughly enjoyed watching the relationship of the angels with Yune. The spiritual journey that they make helps me reflect on my own personal spiritual journey and my need to "wait for Christ". I didn't realize that parts of the Muslim faith paralleled the Christian faith. This is a great summer read!
★★★★★ Crystal Steele Joyce, Winston-Salem, North Carolina

The Gospel of Damascus is a beautiful book, beautiful in its prose and uplifting in its message. The chapter titled "The Gospel of Damascus" is particularly striking in its message. It is hard to describe what feelings this book invoked in me, I felt as though it was more of an experience than an exercise in reading. I will keep this book along with other books that I refer to time and again when I need some guidance in my life as I, too, "wait for Christ."
★★★★★ Joan Scholla, Dunmore, Pennsylvania

The Gospel of Damascus is the first novel, that I am aware of, that is written by a Syrian and perhaps by an Arab author which categorically condemns the Holocaust (I speak here as a Palestinian scholar who is very familiar with contemporary fiction by Arab and Muslim authors). Not only does *The Gospel of Damascus* condemn the Holocaust, but it also makes attempting to save Jews from the Nazis a prerequisite for being selected by God for the most special mission of all: receiving the Christ.
★★★★★ Yasir Sakr, Ph.D., Jordan University of Science and Technology, Irbid, Jordan

An excellent fictional account of the events leading to the coming of the Christ in Damascus. Transcending religions and denominations, we are drawn into a realm of celestials who lead and guide humans to the Will of the Divine. I simply couldn't put this one down! I give this book Five Stars and a big Thumbs Up!
★★★★★ Cynthia Henry, Ronceverte, West Virginia

This is my maiden literary journey with Omar Imady, and what a wonderful journey it was! He masterfully weaves his way between the human and the spiritual world so the reader can experience the angels in our midst that we encounter daily or just know their presence with us. As I read some of the opening pages, I remembered the novels written by Frank Perretti and how he also blended the natural and spiritual entities we encounter daily. There are many surprises also within these pages that keep the reader moving through, wanting more!
★★★★ Gertrude Hutchinson, Altamont, New York

This book is a very well written and entertaining story. On first glance it reads like a fantasy story with its angel-like beings but if you let the story enter your thoughts and actually start to think about it you learn that it is much more. For me it was an eyeopener about my approach to religion - and that is something you did not expect from a novel. I just can't say more for it is more to me. Many thanks!
★★★★ Oliver Fitzner, Leun, Germany

The Gospel
of Damascus

A Novel

For information, contact
MSI Press
1760-F Airline Highway, #203
Hollister, CA 95023

Cover designed by Carl Leaver

Library of Congress Control Number 2011944902

ISBN: 9781933455105

Acknowledgements

This novel would not have seen the light had it not been for the love and support of my special companions who know their place in my heart and the extent of my appreciation.

My affair with MSI Press began in 2005. I discovered then a number of individuals who are not only dedicated professionals, but who also possess a very distinct sensibility; one that I have become addicted to working with. So to Betty, Carl and Geri – thank you for the trust it takes to perpetuate this affair.

Dedication

To the guide of my heart – in hope and faith that you will be holding my hand as I cross to the other side.

"Behold, out of Syria will I begin to call together a new Jerusalem." — Epistula Apostolorum

I. In Search of a Fire Horse

Omar Imady

1

My name is Raqeem, one of eight angels entrusted with the task of facilitating God's design on earth. On the eve of the return of the Anointed One, seven seals were broken and a fire horse was sculpted by the words of golden scrolls. I was a witness to these events and I have been honored with the task of sharing with all the wonders that my eyes have seen.

❖

The *barzakh* is the Transient Partition, a cosmic sphere where angels having earth-related instructions abide. It is also the place where departed human souls are kept until the Day of Judgment. At the end of each Hebrew century, eight angels are sent from the *barzakh* to replace the eight who have completed their mission on earth. These angels are called the Guardians of the Design. My seven companions and I arrived on earth moments after sunset on Thursday the 1st of Tishri, 5701, which corresponds with the 20th of September, 1940, and the 1st of Ramadan, 1359. We are scheduled to be retrieved from earth on Saturday, the 1st of Tishri, 5801, or the 8th of September, 2040, and the 1st of Ramadan, 1462.

Though we have been endowed with human forms, we neither eat nor drink. Yet, we can experience pain and joy, laughter and tears, the sacred gifts to the children of Adam. We are protected from death, but not from its instruments. Our base is Mount Hermon, the original gate to heaven as testified by *The Book of Enoch*. Each of us has been entrusted with the secrets of a sacred quality, as reflected by our very names. Mine, Raqeem or inscription, signifies that my gift is weaving seemingly unrelated segments, as letters are woven into words or sounds are arranged into music.

For nearly twenty-six years, the tasks we were entrusted with were mostly related to crises taking place in various parts of the world. But my companions and I longed for a mission that was of a very different type, a mission that prepared the earth for a dramatic event that would have significant impact on the nature and intensity of human spirituality. But we were all too aware of the fact that such missions were very infrequent and that numerous past members of the Guardians of the Design have arrived on earth and departed without having been honored with such a task. But then suddenly Wahi arrived.

Wahi is not one of us. Not only is he higher in rank, but he is also our link to the Divine Will, a grand go-between, if you like. Everything we help unfold, every move we make during our stay on this planet is inspired by messages conveyed to us by Wahi. When Wahi arrived from the Seventh Sphere we all knew it was important. It had to be important. Though none of us have been invited there, it was quite clear that it was a place where important decisions were made and conveyed. Well, perhaps not made, but definitely conveyed. When Wahi drew near it always felt like wind and light, a strange combination, almost like an electric breeze. His voice, both warm and distant, was consistent with his sense of presence. "Be sure to open each scroll in its designated time," he said, as he handed me a wooden box that contained golden scrolls, reserved for the most important of missions entrusted to us. 'Periodic Unfolding,' the technical term for what Wahi was emphasizing, meant not only that this was an extremely important message, but also that not even I, the angel entrusted with overseeing missions from on-high, would know its true nature until the very end. I watched Wahi disappear in the brilliant sky above Mount Hermon and I carried the scrolls to my cave.

The wooden box is made from branches of the *sidrah* or the Lote Tree, which marks the extreme limits of the Seventh Sphere. I raised the box to my face and inhaled its sacred scent. Inside the box, seven cylinders were neatly placed. The golden scrolls are placed within these glass cylinders. You know the time is right to break a cylinder when it begins to glow, almost like a light bulb, but far more beautifully. One was already glowing when I opened the box. To break a cylinder, you must hold it with both hands and apply pressure on the middle point. It's made in such a way that when pressure is applied, it breaks as though it was perfectly cut with an electric blade. The first cylinder contained two golden scrolls with numbers on each to indicate which should be opened first. Though I was aware that these thin sheets of gold cannot be torn or broken, I was very careful when I unrolled scroll number one. The following words were incised:

A fire horse will be born in the city of Christ to a Huguenot womb and an Uzbek Knight.

This was not a riddle, not intentionally at least. There was no expectation that I would regard it as difficult to understand. The choice of words in these messages reflected what the Divine Will regarded as important, the most essential elements, as it were. This said, I rarely found these messages easy to understand and this particular message was no exception. I had to follow the clues and the first was the fire horse. I knew that the fire horse was the name of one of the years in the Chinese calendar, but I felt there was a lot more to find out. And so, it was time to meet Fei.

When we, the Guardians of the Design, travel, our destination hastens to meet us. We take one step and we suddenly are where we intend to be. A few humans have been blessed with this gift. In Jewish tradition they are known as *kefitzat ha-aretz*, or those for whom earth jumped. As the Rabbis have taught: "For three did the earth shrink: Eliezer, Abraham's servant, our father Jacob, and Abishai the son of Zeruiah ..." In the mystic Islamic tradition, they are known as *ahl al-khitwa*, or the people of the step.

We can also pull people into behaving in certain ways. But this is something we do our best to avoid because people vary in how open they are to being pulled. The extent to which their behavior reflects what we intend them to do is rarely a perfect match. But tonight is different. The man I wanted to meet had perfected the art of being open to angelic pulls. In one step I am in Hangzhou, a Chinese city not too far from Shanghai. I walk into Louwailou, or Tower Beyond Tower, a restaurant overlooking West Lake. And I'm not at all surprised to find Fei sitting inside with a smile on his face.

"So you wanted to see me. I ordered, Shrimp with Dragon Well Green Tea. No one should go through life without having tasted this. You still insist on this no eating policy."

"If I could eat, Fei, I most certainly would not eat shrimp!"

When engaging with humans, we take on various disguises. Our features change at the very moment we envision the person we would like to become. Only with a select few, do we present ourselves as who we really are, angels in human form. Fei was one such exception, but if he were to seriously contemplate sharing our secret with anyone, his memories of our encounters would be instantaneously erased.

"So, Raqeem, I suspect you need some insights on Chinese astronomy?"

"Yes I do, Fei. Please tell me, is the year of the Fire Horse special in any way?"

Fei was a very knowledgeable and eloquent man. I was introduced to him by Mizan, the angel entrusted with the secrets of wisdom and one of my companions on Mount Hermon. Fei's entire world revolved around astronomy and his openness to me made him move quickly to the very points I was interested in.

"Unlike the year of the Horse which takes place every twelve years, the year of the Fire Horse takes place every sixty years. The last year of the Fire Horse was 1906. The next will start a week from today, January 21, 1966, and will end on February 8, 1967."

"Interesting!"

"Children born in the year of the Fire Horse are, to put it simply, extreme horses. They have all the qualities of a child born in the year of the Horse, individualism, love of freedom, hatred of mediocrity, but in a highly accentuated manner. The result is a dangerous creature destined to become famous or infamous, a bearer of tragedy or spectacular fortune. But you see my friend, who wants to take such a risk? This is why some women due to give birth soon are actually planning to have an abortion."

The thought of aborting the gift of a child made me cringe.

"Anything else I should know?"

"Oh yes," he said as he reached for his glass of Shaoxing wine, "fire horses are most dangerous when in love. Whatever self control they are able to practice, it all vanishes when colliding with the passion that love unleashes in them."

In naturally camouflaged caves circling the summit and connected by a network of passageways, my seven companions and I abide. Four of my companions have been given a female physical form. Risha, entrusted with the secrets of subtlety and seduction; Sakinah, entrusted with the secrets of spiritual comfort; Rahma, entrusted with the secrets of love; and Nur, entrusted with the secrets of spiritual change. The remaining three have taken on, as I have, a male physical form. Sur, entrusted with the secrets of law and frameworks; Asa, entrusted with the secrets of lineage and authority; and, finally, Mizan, entrusted with the secrets of balance and wisdom.

Mount Hermon is almost always cold, and in January, heavy snow is a regular occurrence. My home is a beautifully hidden cave. When I'm here, it's usually because I want to contemplate my next move. I reached for the first scroll and read the message again. *A fire horse will be born in the city of Christ …* What is the city of Christ? There must be a deeper meaning to this. I knew I needed help again.

Damascus, like all major cities, is home to forty men and women whose hearts are so pure that they are capable of balancing the darkness of all other hearts in the city. The forty are called *abdal*, or the substitutes, because when one dies, she or he is immediately substituted by another, a process that stops only before the world comes to an end. Amongst the forty is a Reformer who is tasked with diagnosing and prescribing the cure for the most important spiritual disease of his or her age. The forty should not be confused with the seventy *tzadikim*, or righteous ones, who are *abdal* of a higher order and are known to God alone. The hearts of the *tzadikim* carry not a specific city, but rather the earth as a whole. Amongst them are the four *awtad*, or the pegs, and the *qutb*, or the pole. Together, they form an invisible tent, as it were protecting the world from itself!

Under various disguises, I came to know all the Damascene forty and when one of them died, I was often informed by Wahi of his or her replacement. Rabbi Eliezer, a Damascene Jew, had such a heart. He knew me as a rich North African Jew who visited Damascus often. "Yusuf," he would repeat to me, "I will be the last Rabbi of this synagogue. After me, this place will be visited as though it was a museum." Rabbi Eliezer lived in the Jewish Quarter, a walking distance from his synagogue. The sun was about to set when I knocked at his door. A servant with a small colorful scarf on her head greeted me and led me into the courtyard. Moments later Rabbi Eliezer arrived. It was slightly cold, but still pleasant.

"Yusuf, what a wonderful surprise. You disappear until I say, Yusuf will never come back, only to appear until I say Yusuf will never depart! Another business trip I assume. Sit, sit my friend."

A small fountain added a gentle touch to the already serene atmosphere of this Damascene courtyard.

"Rabbi, I was wondering if you could help me with something."

I had not asked Rabbi Eliezer's help before this and he was clearly surprised and intrigued.

"Help? And how can someone like me help someone like you?"

"I was wondering Rabbi, where is the city of Christ located?"

Rabbi Eliezer seemed like I had just asked the one question he never imagined I could possibly ask.

"City of Messiah? Where did you hear about this?"

It was clear from the Rabbi's face that I had raised a very serious subject.

"I overheard a discussion and there just seemed to be so much confusion on where exactly it is located, and I said to myself, Rabbi Eliezer would surely know."

"There is no confusion my friend. The city of the Messiah is Damascus."

"Damascus?"

"Yes my friend, Damascus it is. Most of us rabbis know this. And most of us don't like the idea. What is Damascus after all to be honored in this way? What is Damascus to be chosen over Jerusalem? But *The Book of Zechariah* was clear. Its words leave no doubt. Some rabbis tried to find a way around this. But it's all creative logic, you know. The Messiah will appear in Damascus."

Rabbi Eliezer paused for a minute, as though trying to make sure this was the right thing to do, and then said: "I have something for you. I will get it. Wait here."

Rabbi Eliezer returned after a few moments carrying a small book which appeared as though it had not been opened in a very long time.

"Yusuf, take this. I wrote it years ago and sent it to my friend, Rabbi Isaac of Aleppo. It will answer all of your questions on why Damascus is the city of Christ."

"Thank you Rabbi, thank you."

"Well you must excuse me now, but I have an important visit to make."

"Yes of course, thank you for all your help."

❖

Back in my cave, I reflect on what I've come to know so far. A child will be born in Damascus sometime between now and February next year. Who is this child? I reread the scroll:

A fire horse will be born in the city of Christ to a Huguenot womb and an Uzbek Knight.

"So what do you think Risha?" I ask upon realizing she was standing right behind me. "What is a Huguenot womb, Risha?"

"So now you decide to share. Whatever happened to, 'Raqeem reads and Raqeem weaves, and we only help on demand'?"

"Well, that's the way it's supposed to be. But when the angel of subtlety decides to get involved, there isn't much I can do! So what do you think?"

"The womb must refer to his mother. She must be a descendant of Huguenots. If I'm not mistaken, Huguenots were French Protestants. So perhaps this woman is French or of French ancestry. Somehow she meets and marries a man from Damascus who is a descendant of an Uzbek knight."

"Not bad Risha. But how do I find a woman whose ancestors centuries ago belonged to a French Protestant movement?"

"Well look, the fact that she is descended from Huguenots is probably one of the major traits that qualified her to be the mother of this child. But as far as your attempt to find her, all you really need to know is which European countries, in addition to France, are most identified with Huguenots."

"And if she is an American?"

"Then we look for an American whose ancestors emigrated from that European country. See, it's very simple. Just go find a good book."

I fell in love with the Suzzallo library during a brief stay in Seattle. A young girl had been kidnapped and her ancestors were so highly regarded by God that I was sent, along with Asa, to ensure she was freed and returned to her parents. We found her in a garage outside of Seattle. Her kidnapper was apparently about to disrobe the poor girl when he found us suddenly staring at him. Asa got so carried away that he immediately struck the man on his head. That same evening, after the girl had been reunited with her parents, I found the library and climbed up the marble staircase leading to the Graduate Reading Room, sixty-five feet in height, with Tudor style arches spanning the sides. When it's open for visitors, lighting is provided by beautiful chandeliers. But I had arrived after hours. Breaking into libraries is not a very common angelic ritual but, unlike Asa, I just couldn't leave Seattle without researching the young girl's family. I had to know what it was exactly that made her so important. It turned out it was her maternal great grandmother who was responsible for the family's high spiritual rank. She had devoted her life to the orphans of Seattle, taking young children off the streets and providing them with a safe shelter. Her great granddaughter, in turn, was protected and returned to the safety of her home. How poetic is the Divine Will?

Tonight, my trip to the Graduate Reading Room had a very different objective. As it rained outside, I drowned myself in *A Thirst for Freedom: The Story of the Huguenots*. An hour later, I picked up another book *Stories of Huguenot Survivors*. This I completed shortly after dawn. I stared at the stained glass, now penetrated by numerous beams of light, and willed myself back to Mount Hermon.

"So what did you find out?"

"Well, France is clearly the key word. But I got distracted."

"Distracted?"

"Yes. I came across this story and I don't know why but I kept reading it over and over again."

"Tell me."

"There's this man, a doctor by profession. His name was William Rippon. He escapes Paris during the St. Bartholomew's Day massacre when thousands of Huguenots were killed. He traveled first to England, then Scotland and, finally, settled in Lisbon. In the early 19th century, one of his descendants, Matthew, is said to have suffered from strange illusions."

"How so?"

"Well, it appears he became convinced that his mission was to prepare the world for the Second Coming."

"Of Christ?"

"You can imagine how that was received. His father was so worried about him that he put him on a boat and sent him ..."

"To America?"

"Yes, this man's descendants, the Rippon family, settled mostly in New Rochelle, a town not too far from New York City."

"I can see why you got distracted. Maybe you are right. Maybe the Huguenot womb is descended from Matthew."

"I didn't say this was my theory."

"But it is. Well, look, if she is in Damascus, I promise you, I will find her."

"How will you go about it?"

"Well, first, you are going to have to help. You see, we need to know how many Damascene men who live in Damascus are married to foreign women. Say you find thirty. I can't imagine there's more than thirty! Then, on the basis of your information, we can start eliminating some of these women."

"At the very least, we can eliminate those who are not pregnant. The woman we are looking for is already pregnant or about to get pregnant. By May, if she's not pregnant, she's not the one we are looking for."

"So, get me a list, and I'll take it from there."

I'm at the Immigration and Passport Directorate. A small building full of foreigners seeking permission to stay in Syria and Syrians seeking permission to leave Syria, not to mention lots and lots of cigarette smoke! What I want to know is very specific: the names and nationalities of foreign women, American and European, residing in Damascus because they are married to Syrians. I approach a man in uniform. Either it's my expensive looking suit or my inner pull or both, but he walks towards me as though waiting to hear my instructions.

My request is written on a piece of paper. I place it in his hand. He stares at it for a few seconds and nods his head.

I returned at two in the afternoon. The building now was almost empty. Though thirty minutes were left before official hours were over, most employees had already left. But my officer was solemnly standing near his desk. Was he waiting for me? He handed me the list. I smiled and thanked him, but he only stared at me.

⁘

"So Risha, since you seem addicted to my cave, why don't you help out. There are forty-six names on this list! Here we have eight British women, six Belgians, seven Danes, eleven Russians, and fourteen Americans! Where do we go from here?"

"Well, let's see. They must have some type of get together. So, I'll just be the latest addition to this club, a foreign woman who's very lonely and eager for some real coffee and good conversation."

"I agree. But try to look a bit less pretty. The more you make them jealous, the less likely it is that they are going to confess their ancestry to you."

"Raqeem, you actually sound flirtatious! The problem is, my very favorite angel, no matter what I do, I'll still be the prettiest."

Risha was indeed beautiful. Petite. Long hair, the color of light nutmeg and her eye color shifting from brown to green and everything in between. But it was her sense of presence that moved me the most. Like her very name, she carried with her a sweet ticklish feeling, but not in a physical way, if that makes any sense.

It was a Saturday morning when Risha walked into the house of the Qadri family. She got the phone numbers of some of the American women on the list by contacting the

American embassy. She phoned them and they quickly welcomed her to their next coffee and apple pie gathering.

Later that night, Risha was full of stories on foreign women in Damascus, but most importantly, she was convinced she had identified the Huguenot womb.

"OK. So, I walk into this apartment and there they were with their pretty small dresses; the foreign wives of Damascus. I introduced myself as Vicki and ..."

"Vicki?"

"Yup. It has something royal about it. And they take me in and start showering me with advice on how to survive life without vanilla extract, strawberries, and most importantly, regular butter! Then suddenly, this woman walks in with dark chestnut long hair and those eyes, how can I explain those eyes? It was as though all that love of freedom and that amazing spirit of protest that the Huguenots once had was emanating from those eyes."

"Risha, get to the point please."

"OK. OK. We were first introduced. Her name is Jane. Jane Rippin."

"You must be kidding. That sounds like a definite variation of Rippon!"

"She has one daughter. Her husband works for the government. They met at Columbia University. And guess what? His name is Jawdat Bukhari. Get it? Bukhari from Bukhara; a very important city in ... Uzbekistan. It's like it's all suddenly unraveling. But that wasn't all."

"I'm listening. I'm listening."

"So we start talking and I notice how she's avoiding eating anything. "You don't like apple pie?" I ask casually. And she answers, "I don't like anything this morning." "How far along?" I ask, looking at her stomach. "Three months. And how long have you been in Damascus?" she asked, quickly changing the subject. So, there you have it. Three months. Due date should be around July 1966!"

"Risha, I must confess…"

"Wait, there's more. I tell her there's something Irish about her. And she says, her father once told her that their family can be traced back to France and Ireland. She's even heard that the first of her ancestors to immigrate to America was a very religious man who was forced to leave Ireland to escape persecution."

"Amazing, that must be Matthew."

"Perhaps, but I have a feeling that now that you know all you need to know, you are about to cut me off. I will not like that. No, don't look away. I'm serious. It's not smart to upset an angel with my talents."

"I have no such intention."

❖

2

The Zahiriyah National Library is located northwest of the Grand Mosque of Damascus and was founded in the 13th century by Sultan Baybars. Baybars was the antithesis of Saladin and is known for his ruthless re-conquests of Crusader-held land. He is buried in the library under a majestic rose dome. Damascus may indeed be the city of Christ, but it is also the city of rose domes. Rose domes often built over the tombs of saints, are scattered all over Damascus. Damascenes seem so accustomed to their presence that they don't quite realize how unusual they are, their color in particular. On days when rain is followed by sunshine, they are truly beautiful, especially from above.

I was at the Zahiriyah because I had to know why the Bukhari family was selected, not just out of curiosity, but also to silence any possible doubt that I may still have. Muslim historians were possessed with writing *kutub al- rijal*, or the books which contained brief biographies of all the important men, and at times women, who lived in a specific Islamic century. Some were general works and others were more city-specific. In the grand Baybars Hall, I found a collection of works on scholars and notables of Damascus. They began with the 16th century and continued all the way to the present.

Kasbay, the father of Imad al-Din Bukhari was a soldier in the army of the Mamluk prince Janberdi al-Ghazali, the last Mamluk ruler of Damascus. Al-Ghazali had initially joined the Ottomans, but after the death of Sultan Salim in 1520, he proclaimed himself the Sultan of Syria, only to be subsequently killed by the army of Suleiman the Magnificent that was sent to reclaim Damascus for the Ottomans. Kasbay survived the battle and retreated to a small house in the Anaba suburb of Damascus. For his son, Imad al-Din, he chose a very different path, the study of Islamic jurisprudence. Imad al-Din became an important scholar of the *hanafi* school of law. Sunni Islam has four schools of law, *hanafi, shafi'i, maliki,* and *hanbali.* The Mamluks had favored the *shafi'i* school of law, but the Ottomans were *hanafi* to the core and Imad al-Din was riding the wave of the time. His son Hamid surpassed his father and became the *mufti,* or the highest religious authority, of Damascus, a position which was to be later occupied by six additional Bukharis. By the 18th century, the Bukharis had turned from scholarship to managing the extensive wealth that their ancestors had acquired, since the Sultans were in the habit of bequeathing entire villages to important religious scholars. By the early twentieth century when Jawdat was born, most of the wealth was lost. Jawdat was born to an aristocratic but impoverished family. His graduate education in economics on a government scholarship at New York University and his rise as an important technocrat in the Syrian government was in a sense a rebirth of the Bukharis in the modern age.

The Bukharis were clearly an interesting family, but I had not come across anything that would decisively explain why they were selected. Their religious scholars were important, but I found nothing beyond intellectual contributions and successful careers. And then, in the midst of what should have been the phase of Bukhari decline when even their wealth had started to shrink, I came across the biography of Ahmad Bukahri, a Damascene notable who died in 1888. According to his biographical note, he was married to an Abyssinian woman who was once his house servant, not a very common event in nineteenth-century Damascus. Even more interesting is the fact that Ahmad lived in Qaymariya, very near to Bab Tuma, or the Thomas Gate, a largely Christian neighborhood in Damascus. This is important because in 1860, the sectarian killings that had started in Mount Lebanon between Maronites and Druze arrived in Damascus. Muslim mobs attacked Christian neighborhoods, killing many and destroying numerous houses.

A few Muslims stood up to the angry mobs and protected as many Christians as they could. Abd al-Qadir al-Jazairi, the Algerian prince who was living in exile in Damascus, along with his personal guards, saved many Christians and was later acknowledged for his actions by the West. But Ahmad Bukhari, the great grandfather of Jawdat Bukhari, didn't have guns or guards and his attempt to protect his neighbors was not acknowledged by anyone. Yet, he opened his home to Christians fleeing the mobs, risking his life in the process and placing his own family in danger. Ahmad's biography even states that some pregnant Christian women gave birth at Ahmad's home. One of the two children who were born there became a medical doctor who was known to never accept money from any patient of the Bukhari family.

I smiled when I came across Ahmad's biography. Angels know when they have found what they are searching for even if they have difficulty rationalizing it to others. Perhaps it was the very fact that if we take into account Ahmad's African wife, the fire horse embodies four continents: Asia and Africa, through his paternal line; and Europe and America, through his maternal line. Or perhaps it was Ahmad's willingness to go out of his way to protect a group of people who belonged to another faith. This was a rare type of kindness. Not the type expressed towards members of one's own, but rather the type that is expressed towards those who belong to a different group at precisely the time when they are most vulnerable. Like the story of Matthew Rippon, Ahmad

Bukhari's biography was just what I needed to cast aside any iota of doubt that the Bukharis were indeed the paternal line of the fire horse.

✢

3

Once I had identified the parents of this child, I knew that I needed new instructions. There were two scrolls in the first cylinder. One had been fulfilled. It was time to open the second:

Dove will be the name of the new born moon and Sakinah will be there when he arrives at noon.

"Dove. Interesting. What does that correspond to?"

"I'm clueless. Maybe it's just a metaphor?"

"Or maybe it's Hebrew?"

"Why would it be Hebrew?"

"Think Biblically, Risha."

"I don't know how to think Biblically, Mr. Raqeem!"

"The question is who among the Biblical prophets had a name that means something like dove?"

"I couldn't guess even if our whole mission depended on it."

"Asa would know. Let's pay him a visit."

Asa's cave was further up the summit. When we walked in, he was reading a large book. He looked as royal and handsome as ever. In one of the corners I noticed his scepter, the symbol of his authority.

"Asa, we're very sorry to interrupt. We just have a quick question. Were any of the Biblical prophets named Dove?"

"Jonah."

"Jonah, the one who was swallowed by the whale?"

"I'm not sure he would like to be characterized as such, but yes, Jonah, the one who succeeded in converting his city to monotheism."

He said this and, as though to signal that the conversation was now over, he reopened his book and drifted away. Back in my cave, I asked Risha:

"So how do we inspire Jawdat and Jane to name their son Yunus, the Arabic version of Jonah?"

"That's easy, you seduce them!"

"Risha!?"

"Listen, I'll come up with a story about this amazing man named Yunus and share it with Jane on our next coffee and pie gathering."

"How will you make it seductive?"

"I don't make things seductive. Everything I do is seductive. Period."

⬥

"I opened the Qur'an the other day, an English translation, and it was all about Jonah. It's pronounced beautifully in Arabic, Yunus. And the story. How do I put it? You must admit, there's something very special about the idea of a man inside a whale. It's like the closest you get to being in a womb."

Risha looked at Jane and smiled briefly. A few women laughed, but Jane was clearly very interested and hoped that Risha wouldn't stop.

"It's dark; it's humid. I wonder if he could hear the whale's heart beating."

Laura, from Pittsburgh, interrupted, "My husband told me once that he was actually able to hear the fish praising God in the sea."

Emily, from Mansfield, added, "What's so beautiful about Jonah is that even though he does something not very proper, he still seems to be the only Prophet of that age to actually succeed in converting the city he was sent to." Jane nodded her head. Risha rejoined the conversation, "Yes, Emily, it's almost like if you want to succeed, you have to be like Yunus. You have to be placed in a womb not once, but twice." Now all the women in the room were laughing, all but Jane who seemed to have suddenly thought of an idea that was very pleasing to her.

The caves of the Guardians of the Design all have a large screen fixed to one of their walls. When we want to observe what's taking place anywhere on earth, all we have to do is sit in front of this screen and project our hearts towards a specific place or person. The screen is immediately brought to life by very vivid imagery. When our hearts are projected elsewhere, it's as if one flips a channel and the imagery is changed instantaneously. And so that evening, Risha and I sat on my green velvet couch and watched Jawdat return home from work, late as usual, and walk into the bedroom. Jane, who was lying on the bed waiting for him, smiled and informed him that, yes, his father may have been named Idris, and yes, it may be the custom here to name sons after their grandfather, still, if the child she's carrying is a boy, his name will be nothing other than Yunus.

"Yunus? But Jane, you can't even pronounce it correctly!"

"I already figured out a way around that, a nickname."

"A nickname? What nickname?"

"I'll let you know. Goodnight!"

Jane said this, turned off the reading light to her right, and closed her eyes. And as she slowly drifted into sleep, it seemed as though her mind was constantly trying to visualize what it was like for her unborn child to be inside her womb.

A major solar x-ray flare was observed on the 7th of July, 1966 with an 81.8-second time resolution. Something was about to happen. I knew this because solar flares indicate an important event is imminent. I walked into Risha's cave which she had transformed into a large wardrobe! She was standing in front of a mirror, trying hats on.

"Since when did you visit my cave?"

"Listen, you need to phone Jane. We need to find out if she's in labor."

"I'm way ahead of you. I've been phoning everyday for the last week. No one is answering. I phoned a friend of hers and I found out Jane and her family are in Latakia."

"Latakia? They can't be in Latakia. The child is about to be born. I want them back."

"Well, you can try pulling."

"We both have to pull."

"OK. I just hope Jane is the type that responds nicely or should I say predictably to being pulled. Have you informed Sakinah?"

"Yes, don't worry about Sakinah. If the child is born in Damascus, she'll be there. She's been a nurse in the Italian Hospital for three months now."

"Leave it to my Raqeem."

That afternoon, on Thursday the seventh of July, Jane suddenly informs everyone that if she doesn't get to Damascus in the next few hours, she's going to have a grand American nervous breakdown. The announcement was made over coffee during what Jawdat mistakenly believed was a serene moment.

The road from Latakia to Damascus takes around five hours. But Jawdat's driver, Abu Hadi, was driving nearly 70 miles an hour and when he wasn't, Jane would begin to scream, "I need to be in Damascus. I want to give birth in Damascus, I have to be in Damascus."

The Gospel of Damascus

On Friday, the 8th of July, in the hottest part of the day, the hottest month of the year and in the year of the Fire Horse, Yunus, or Yune as he will come to be known, was born in Damascus, the city of Christ. Sakinah was the first to carry him. She blew a prayer at his face and gave him to Jawdat who recited the Muslim call for prayer in his right ear and then placed him in his mother's arms.

❖❖❖

Omar Imady

II. When a Child Falls in Love

Omar Imady

1

Back at Mount Hermon, I found Risha waiting for me. She had a ruby dress on and was lying on my couch.

"We are in a ruby mood?"

"I'm always in a ruby mood when a child is born! I have a feeling one of the scrolls is ready to be opened."

"A feeling, you say. Let's just open the box and see."

Risha was of course, right. We had completed the first task and we now needed new instructions. I broke the seal. Like the first cylinder, the second contained two scrolls. Risha opened the first scroll and read its message:

As Merriam was once to Moses, his sister will be to him.
Rahma – 8 years.

"A love story," Risha said with a big smile.

We both knew that the presence of Rahma amounted to the birth of a love story.

"Yes, but does Yune have a sister?"

"Yes, I mentioned to you once that the Bukharis had a daughter. Jane shared this with me on the first day I met her. Why are you asking?"

"Miriam was the sister of Moses. She loved her brother so much that she followed him to the house of Pharaoh. Yune and his sister seem destined to have a similar relationship."

"I have goose bumps."

I smiled at the thought of Risha experiencing such a human sensation.

"So our Yune is meant to be introduced to life through a love story with his sister, the sister that neither one of us know anything about."

"Well I will make sure I meet her on my next visit to Jane's home."

"Good. I will contact Rahma. She can pose as a house servant."

"Yes, and I will recommend her to Jane. You know she cannot resist my ideas." She said this with a smile and walked out of my cave.

✛

Yune did indeed have a sister. Her name was Maryam, Arabic for Mary, and she was around nine years older than Yune. Unlike her mother's eyes which radiated freedom and vitality, Maryam's eyes evoked depth and spirituality. Risha introduced Rahma to Jane as Suad, the ideal house servant and baby sitter. Jane spoke of a job she was offered prior to giving birth. She never thought it would be possible with a new born baby but now she was going to reconsider.

And so the seeds for the frequent presence of Rahma were planted in the Bukhari home. In the shadow of the angel entrusted with the secrets of love, Yune's love for his sister grew and, like Fei had once predicted, Yune was intolerable to everyone when separated from his love. When Maryam managed to escape unnoticed to see a friend or just to have time alone, Yune, the once eager-to-please child, would become tense, then rude, then loud and finally, if Maryam's disappearance lasted more than two hours, violent, but only toward objects. His Lego structures would break apart under the blows of his hands. Once he even hit a glass window which shattered instantly all over the floor. And there was really nothing one could do except, of course, find Maryam and beg her to hurry back home.

The Gospel of Damascus

When Yune was around six, his father became an important official in the Syrian government, the Minister of Economy. He was a technocrat though, and he kept away from the corrupt and those addicted to power. Jawdat lacked all of the qualifications necessary to reach such a post in the Syria of the 1970s. He belonged to a *sunni* aristocratic family when most important officials came from rural backgrounds; he was committed to his faith, when most officials were extreme secularists, and not only was he educated in the west, he was married to an American at a time when the Syrian government was openly hostile to America and everything associated with it. Jawdat would not have been appointed to this post had it not been for a peculiar event. The Minister of Defense, who was later to become the President of Syria, needed someone to help him with a course in Economics. Jawdat was selected and by the time the course was over, he had left a very favorable impression on the general. And so in 1971, when Jawdat was offered a UN post outside of Syria, he received a phone call in the middle of the night from the Presidential Palace asking him to stay because … his country needed him. Jawdat felt alienated throughout the years he spent working with the Syrian government. During bad days, and there were many, when his exposure to just how corrupt and violent some of these officials he was surrounded by could be, he would put himself to sleep with this comforting thought: "Wasn't Joseph a Minister of Economy who worked for Pharaoh; wasn't he, the pure monotheist, surrounded by Egypt's cultic polytheism; and yet, didn't he perform in a manner that pleased his God and made his father and mother proud? I will follow his example to the very end."

Yune understood that his father was an important man and this enhanced his own sense of identity. But Yune was mostly consumed by his love. It was not a romantic love of course. But it wasn't the usual type of love brothers held for their sisters either. Yune simply felt an overwhelming sense of peace and warmth around Maryam. Nothing else gave him this feeling. It was that simple. He needed her around him to feel normal.

Walks were one of the most common rituals of this love story. The main walk was on Sunday even though it wasn't a day off in Syria. With Rahma a few steps behind them, Maryam would hold her brother's hand and embark on a search for four-leaf clovers. Yune's face would almost disappear into the grass as he earnestly searched and searched. The actual clover meant nothing to him. It was Maryam's pleasure that he sought, the smile he imagined she would have if he were to find this magical plant.

Other walks focused on jasmine flowers. Many Damascene homes are surrounded by jasmine trees. Maryam and Yune would pick up the jasmine flowers that had fallen to the ground and place them in a small paper bag. When their bag was full, they would rush home and sit on Maryam's bed and, with a needle and a white thread, carefully make jasmine necklaces.

Words were also a big part of this story. Maryam loved poetry, and, in turn, Yune fell in love with verbal art. A few verses she once wrote on a card she had taped to her closet were to stay with Yune long after they were to be forgotten by Maryam:

I am a fragment from the foam of the sea.
Destined to give birth to a thousand fragments.
And they are, in turn, destined to give birth to me.

Maryam was a big fan of a Lebanese singer named Fairuz. Every summer, Fairuz's new musical at the Damascus fair was an event anticipated by everyone in the Bukhari family. But while Jane and her husband attended the musical once, Maryam and Yune came back over and over again to the open air theater. The words Fairuz sang were written down carefully by Maryam, and she frequently memorized them and sang them to Yune as she put him to sleep. So much of Fairuz was about waiting. She sang about waiting for the one she loved in summer and in winter, waiting with no expectation of a day when her loved one would arrive. In another musical, Fairuz plays the role of a woman who proclaims that a train will soon arrive. There are no tracks however, and in fact potatoes are being planted at the very site she claims the train will soon arrive! Yet, she holds on to a faith of waiting, a senseless waiting that is almost indifferent to the actual arrival of what is so intensely anticipated. In another musical, she plays the role of a woman wrongly imprisoned for fifteen years. What kept her going during those years in her cell? The experience of waiting, no doubt. One scene in particular left a strong impression on Yune. Fairuz wonders why this man is always intoxicated. And someone answers her, "Because he is afraid that if he was to become sober, he would realize that what he is waiting for will never arrive!"

Yune, in turn, soaked all this in. After all, it was special to Maryam, and all that was special to Maryam was special to him. The irony was that a day would come when Fairuz and her words would mean very little to Maryam. Yet, all that was implanted in Yune during these years of innocent love would stay with him for a lifetime.

Not only were words very important, but everything associated with them as well. Maryam attended the Music Institute of Damascus where she learned how to play the piano. A Syrian man married to a British friend of Jane's was the head of the Institute and he was enchanted with Maryam's musical talents. But Maryam wasn't a dedicated student. She only wanted to learn how to read music well enough to play a few of her favorite classical works, and once this was achieved, she stopped attending lessons altogether. How often would I watch Yune sitting on the bench of the piano next to his sister as she played the "Moonlight Sonata." She even made up a story about it. Something along the lines of a young man who sits beneath the light of the moon waiting for his beloved. Night after night he waits, but no one arrives. On the night the moon completely disappears, she suddenly arrives and the sky glows with the light of her face.

Jane was even more musically talented than her daughter. She played the guitar and the piano and had a beautiful voice. Often, when Maryam was away, Jane would sing Yune's favorite songs to distract him from focusing on his sister's absence. The songs he wanted to hear were always the same, and always in the same order. First, "The Minstrel Boy," followed by "Dona Dona," and "Henry Martin." Finally, he would ask for the song he loved the most which Jane would have to sing at least twice, "The Battle Hymn of the Republic." Jane was careful to sing only those parts that were not inconsistent with Islam's strong stand on unitarian monotheism, thereby omitting references to Jesus as God.

And there was more. Maryam once spoke to Yune about an old man who had a small shop that sold hand-bound notebooks. There, Yune was captivated by the sight of a large notebook, almost half his size, with its dark green leather jacket. When Maryam agreed to buy it for him, Yune felt like he had acquired yet another precious brick needed to build his secret castle. A castle made of words, jasmine necklaces, notebooks and, eventually, a small kitten. A friend of Jane's had a few kittens she wanted to get rid of. And so Yune and Maryam walked to her house, chose the white kitten with the black stripe on its nose, placed it in a small bag and walked back home. Every now and then, Yune would stop and make sure the bag was open enough for the kitten to breathe but not enough for her to jump out.

❖

The Gospel of Damascus

In 1973, a war broke out between Arab countries and Israel. Maryam decided she would volunteer at the public Muwasat Hospital. And so, there was Yune, experiencing a war without Maryam by his side. Every dawn, Israeli warplanes broke the sound barrier over Damascus. The sound of sirens arrived first, waking everyone up in the Bukhari family and forcing them to climb down the stairs to the first floor where Jawdat's sisters lived. In a room believed to be protected because Jawdat's father had so frequently prayed in it, members of the family would gather. But quickly, Yune found himself on his own. His father was at work, his fearless mother with her Huguenot genes was on the roof searching for MIG 21s and Mirage 3s in the October sky; and, most importantly from the standpoint of Yune, Maryam was at the hospital looking after wounded civilians. Even Rahma's visits were no longer as regular because the war had disrupted all normal activities. One day this became so intolerable to Yune that he decided he had to see Maryam at all costs. And so, the moment Jawdat's driver appeared at the house, Yune, with a voice of authority that was mysteriously very convincing, asked the driver to take him to the Muwasat hospital. This took place during a very dangerous part of the day. And when Yune arrived at the hospital, he found Maryam standing near a bed with a wounded man lying on it. When she saw him, she couldn't believe her younger brother was in this very dangerous place. She rushed towards him and slapped him on the face. Yune had just experienced a very special test. Was he willing to be humiliated for his love? But he clearly passed that test. All that mattered to him was that he saw her. She, and everyone else for that matter, could do what they pleased. The driver took him back home, his cheek still red, his eyes still watery, and his lips smiling.

❖

Omar Imady

2

On Yune's eighth birthday, the second scroll of the second cylinder was ready to be opened:

Light will kiss his sister in September, and the child's world will be decorated with blue splendor.
Nur – 2 years & 5 months.

Nur is the angel of sudden change and spiritual conversion. When a change in a spiritual paradigm is needed, Nur arrives on the scene. Nur's cave had a very serene feeling to it. She was meditating on a white bed when I arrived, and, as usual, she had on a white, so very white, headscarf. In all the years I've known her, I don't recall ever seeing her hair. Nur opened her eyes and stared at me as though my sudden arrival had disrupted her tranquility.

"Raqeem, the feeling you carry tells me you've been around Risha a lot lately."

Nur and Risha never quite got along. Their vibes, after all, are so markedly different, yet ironically, very complimentary.

"I must have been invoked by one of your scrolls to be visited by you."

"Yes, you have been engaged. Maryam, a seventeen-year-old girl in Damascus is to experience a spiritual conversion."

"I know all about Maryam, Raqeem."

"You do?"

"Risha tends to share more than you seem to be aware of."

"OK. So what is the plan?"

"I will introduce her to the Daughters of Aaron."

"What?"

"You don't seem to be in touch with spiritual events in Damascus."

Nur was right. I have been so consumed with Yune that even when I'm not directly involved, I spend most of my time watching him in my cave.

"Do you, for example, know who the most recent member of the forty is?"

"..."

"Do you know that this new member is destined to become the next Reformer?"

"..."

"Too much Risha can block your vision. Well, allow me to educate you. Around the time Maryam was born, a woman named Shams began to invite Damascene women to embark on a distinct spiritual path, a path that emphasized learning and education and synthesized modernity and modesty. To those women who were striving for a way of life that was neither secular nor traditional, neither free from religious identity nor subservient to traditional authority, to all such women, the path of Shams was an ideal alternative. Had you been out and about more often, you would have noticed that a new style of dress has emerged in Damascus. In contrast to the miniskirts of Western designers and the black skirt and wimple of Ottoman culture, women who have joined the path of Shams walk dressed in sky blue coats and matching headscarves."

"Wait, did you say blue?"

"Yes, sky blue. Why do you seem surprised?"

"No, no. I just recalled the words of the scroll."

"Share them with me."

Light will kiss his sister in September, and the child's world will be decorated with blue splendor.

"You see how on track I am."

"Yes, please continue with your story about Shams."

"Shams succeeded in capturing the attention of educated, self-actualized women, some of whom come from very elitist families in Damascus, the most susceptible to secularization. Yes, there is something about Shams and her path that is very attractive."

"Seductive?"

"That would be Risha terminology. I told you, you spend too much time with her."

"Continue, Nur."

"They are attracted enough to fight back against all those who try to prevent them from joining her."

"Who tries to prevent them?"

"Men! That's why all of this is so ironic. Men in Damascus either want their women to be liberal and dress according to western norms or to cover and follow very strict religious rules. In both cases, they want to be in control. But women who have embraced the path of Shams are confusing to them; they dress modestly but think and live in the most liberated manner."

"I feel like I've been living on a different planet."

"Or simply watching too much TV with Risha!"

"Stop the sarcasm, please. It doesn't fit your spiritual presence."

"You're right. I apologize."

"So why do you refer to them as Daughters of Aaron?"

"According to Luke, Elizabeth, the mother of John the Baptist belonged to the Daughters of Aaron, an ancient female spiritual order. So too, is the case with women who have embraced the path of Shams. Not only do they dress in a certain way, but they also live in accordance with very strict moral precepts and, listen carefully Raqeem, they regularly practice *zikr*."

"Spiritual meditation."

"That's right. In this sense, they are modern manifestations of the Daughters of Aaron."

"So how come you know so much about them?"

"Because Raqeem, I have joined them."

Nur said this as she reached for a sky blue coat hanging near her bed and placed it over her shoulders.

"Take a good look at me. I am Zainab, one of the many disciples of the breathtaking Shams."

"Very good, Nur. So how do we attract, yes attract, Maryam to the path of Shams?"

"I will knock on her door and drown her world with light! I must wait, however, until September like the message said. By then, the month of Ramadan would have begun. Maryam and her family will be fasting and fasting always has this spiritual effect on people."

"Unless they are frustrated by their nicotine withdrawal symptoms."

"Yes, well I seriously doubt Maryam smokes!"

❖

Outside of the seduction-attraction terminology dispute, tactics used by Risha and Nur are very similar indeed. On Wednesday the 25th of September, which corresponded to the 8th of Ramadan in the Islamic Calendar, I watched as Nur knocked at the door of the Bukhari household. Yune opened the door.

"Is Maryam here?"

Yune looked surprised. This wasn't a friend of his sister.

"Yes, my sister is here."

Nur followed Yune inside. Moments later, Maryam appeared, barefoot and wearing a long green hippie dress. Nur introduced herself as Zainab. She said she had come to ask Maryam if she wanted more than this.

"Excuse me?" Maryam exclaimed. "More than what?"

Nur smiled. And then for over twenty minutes, she described the promise of a way of life that would bring all her raw fragments together, that would make her feel sound and serene.

"I know someone who can teach you how to fly out of here without leaving. I know someone who knows how to weave wings."

Maryam smiled. "Take me to her."

When Nur left, Yune looked confused. He asked his sister who was that woman and what was she talking about.

"Don't worry, Yune. She just wanted to invite me to listen to someone give a talk this evening. You can come with me, if you wish."

"Of course I wish, of course," repeated the eight-year-old.

⁜

That evening, Maryam told her mom she was going to see a friend and that she would be taking Yune with her. Nur was waiting at a nearby street. They walked together from Muhajreen where the Bukharis lived to the prestigious neighborhood of Malki. When they arrived at the house, Nur led them into a large room with a Bohemian crystal chandelier and a large Nain Persian carpet. There were about thirty-five young girls, and they were sitting on all the chairs and spilling over onto the carpet. In the front of the room, there were two chairs, Queen Anne with dark blue velvet covering, and no one was sitting on them.

After taking off their shoes, Maryam and Yune sat on the carpet and waited for something to happen. A few minutes later, two women in coats and scarves entered the room.

Everyone rushed to greet them. One stood out clearly. Her smile radiated her warmth and her eyes sparkled with intelligence. As the girls flocked to her to shake her hand, she asked each about their health, their studies and their families. Yune's eyes moved back and forth from the chandelier to the woman's face as though trying to figure out whether it was the chandelier's crystal that was illuminating the woman's face or whether her face simply lent the chandelier its glow.

Both women sat on the Queen Anne chairs. The one with the glowing face began to speak. Nur whispered in Maryam's ear, "Isn't she beautiful? She's Shams, the one I spoke to you of." Maryam nodded in agreement.

Shams spoke in a strong, melodious voice:

Our path, my daughters, has a location, a base—Damascus. And true, we love our city and our country, but our path transcends all prejudice against people of other nationalities. Our path is a female path, but it respects and loves fathers, brothers, husbands and sons. It holds no grudge against men; it just has no need to prove itself to them. It savors a woman's right to choose her religion, learn her religion, practice her religion, but does not seek separation from men. It savors a woman's financial independence, her right to continue her education and choose a career but never at the emotional expense of jeopardizing her pivotal role in the family. Our path is a spiritual path. Yet it is also a path of servitude: serving our God by serving God's creation. This is not a path that seeks enlightenment from solitude; it is a path that achieves high levels of spirituality from the serving of humankind.

Only moments after Shams had concluded her talk, a young woman walked in the room carrying a tray of tea. Yune seemed to wonder whether or not there was a cup for him and when he was offered one, he was very pleased, not because he wanted to drink tea, but because he wanted to feel that his presence was felt and acknowledged.

As Maryam and Yune walked back home, neither one of them spoke. Yune was seemingly still trying to solve the mystery of the glowing face and Maryam was clearly reflecting on the words of Shams. Maryam didn't sleep that night. The vision of a strong, educated, socially conscious, female spirituality that Shams had shared had overtaken her. She didn't even know how to resist an invitation of this type. When Nur phoned her the next morning, Maryam told her that she had decided to commit herself to the path and that, yes, she would start wearing a headscarf.

❖

"Task accomplished."

"Yes, so it seems. I watched carefully. What happens now Nur?"

"Raqeem, now Maryam's light has been kindled. And now they will all try to put it out. Little do they know that this particular type of light is like a desert plant, the more you try to uproot it, the deeper its roots spread."

❖

Maryam's decision to wear a scarf was a revolutionary act not only in the Bukhari household, but in all the Syrian-foreign families who were friends with the Bukharis. Maryam had demonstrated to all of them that their children, their daughters in particular, were not immune to spiritual seduction, or attraction, as Nur would prefer. And Shams, in turn, had demonstrated that women who have all the qualifications to join the path of secularism, women who are very serious about who they are and what they intend to do in this world, are not only welcome to join this path, they are, in fact, almost created for it.

Maryam's parents, friends and relatives constantly argued with her. Yet, she seldom allowed herself to engage. It really didn't matter to her if she convinced any of them at this point. Yune alone stood by her, but more so out of love than conviction. He hated the idea that his Maryam was under attack. In his large notebook, he documented arguments that would take place between Maryam and her parents and then wrote his own comments:

> "Her only crime is holding onto her scarf ..."
> "They don't have a problem with women who wear bandanas ..."
> "Next time they make her cry, I'm going to show them ..."

Maryam's newly found self reinvented the rituals of Yune's love story with her. Their walks were replaced with driving around poor Damascene neighborhoods in Maryam's new car, a small white Peugeot 101, to distribute food and clothes. Many other Shamsi girls, as they were referred to by Damascenes, came along and the small car was often packed. Images of these poor people left a strong impression on Yune. There was one event in particular that left him mesmerized. Eleven families were given portions from a pot of zucchini in tomato sauce that was placed in the trunk. When they reached the twelfth family, Maryam opened the trunk and uncovered the pot to see how much was left. She was expecting to find it nearly empty, but it was still completely full! Yune regarded such events as the new secrets of his love story. Neither he nor Maryam shared them with anyone else and he just loved it when they were sitting with others and he could whisper to her, as though to confirm that they had a private realm not open to others, "Remember when?"

Words remained an important part of their love, but rather than the words of Fairuz, now they were verses from the Qur'an. Yune's favorite, but on purely musical grounds, was the *Book of TaHa*. There were also many bedtime stories that always had a spiritual message. One such story that would serve to complement Yune's fire horse traits and later become the foundation for a lifestyle that Maryam could not have predicted was the story of Bisher the Barefooted. The story had a simple plot, but it never failed to impress Yune:

> A long time ago, there was a man named Bisher who was very rich and who lived a very extravagant life. One day, an old man knocked his door. One of the servants opened the door and was surprised to see this old man. She asked him what it was he wanted. He answered: "Please ask your master if he had tasted freedom yet?" The servant quickly slammed the door. When she was asked by Bisher who was at the door, she responded that it was a crazy old man asking crazy questions. Bisher was intrigued and insisted on hearing the old man's words. When she repeated them, Bisher seemed to be almost struck by lightning. He ran out of his castle, without even taking the time to put on his shoes, and searched for the old man until he found him. He took hold of his hand and said: "You are right, I have not tasted freedom. Please, teach me how to be free." Bisher didn't return to his castle. From that day on, he abandoned his previous life and never looked back!

And so the days passed. Yune adapted fully to Maryam's new lifestyle and as long as she kept him as a part of her world, he was happy. At one point, Maryam tried to convince

Yune to go to an all male religious talk given by an *imam*, or a Muslim man who leads the prayer at a mosque. Yune agreed to do so for her sake, but after he came back home he told her that he hated every minute of it and that he would never go without her to an event like that again.

In September 1976, Yune found out that Maryam was going to accompany her father on a trip to America. Jawdat was going to attend an International Monetary Fund conference in Washington DC and Maryam would visit her grandmother and aunts in New Rochelle, or so Yune thought. In actuality, the Bukharis were approached by a religious Damascene family whose son was studying medicine in America. Maryam surprised her parents by her willingness to meet him, and so the trip was planned. No one dared to share any of this with Yune, but Jawdat's sisters were not good at keeping secrets. Yune heard enough from his aunts to understand that something was being cooked up that had to do with marriage. Maryam was gone for ten days during which an informal engagement took place.

On the night she returned, Yune's deep love for her was shown in a very sweet way. Though he was asleep when she arrived at home, he woke up upon hearing her voice and asked her to come and give him a hug. When she came close to him, his hands immediately took hold of hers and searched for a ring. When he didn't find one – Maryam had placed it in her purse – Yune smiled and went back to sleep.

But his smile would not last long. A wedding was set for December, and by October, 1976, Yune had understood it all and confronted Maryam. She, in turn, took hold of his shoulders and spoke to him of the man she was going to marry and of how he had long hair. One would have expected Yune to say, "Do you really think I care if he has long, short or no hair at all?" But Yune felt the love radiating from her hands and, for the moment at least, was willing to talk about Sarmad's hair. When Sarmad arrived in Damascus a few days before the wedding, Yune was at the airport. His eyes searched for a man who looked and dressed like a hippie! He even imagined him to be carrying a guitar. But Sarmad was wearing a suit and his hair was average length.

The wedding took place at the Bukhari's home. Hotels were not an option because they served alcohol, and Maryam's path included a strong stand against alcohol-serving establishments. During the wedding, Yune often broke into tears. Not only was his sister getting married, but she was also leaving Damascus the very next day with her husband for America. Life, as he had experienced it so far, was effectively over.

❖❖❖

Omar Imady

III. All Roads Lead to Damascus

Omar Imady

1

There were still tears on my cheek when Risha walked in. She noticed them immediately and her hand reached up to my face and gently wiped them away. A few seconds of bliss. I loved it when she touched my face or played with my hair. It was as close to human intimacy as we angels could get. Almost like the feeling a human child gets when he is suddenly kissed on the cheek by a young girl playing with him in the backyard.

"Why is my Raqeem crying?"

"I was watching a wedding!"

"And I bet you didn't even notice the beautiful dress I was wearing."

"You were there?"

"Of course, I was there. No one danced like I did."

"Danced? With whom?"

"With no one, Mr. Jealous. There were only two males in the entire wedding. Yune, who was most of the time out of sight, and Sarmad, who arrived towards the end. It was a female wedding, very different from the ones that take place in Damascene hotels."

"Weren't you worried about Yune?"

"Worried? I am the antithesis of fear! He'll be fine. It's all going to be OK. It was a cute love story until Nur showed up! Anyway, it's time to move on. I bet there is a cylinder just beaming with light."

Like the previous two, the third cylinder also contained two scrolls. It was as if the first scroll in each cylinder was meant to begin a phase and the second was meant to complete it.

From within the sand dunes, a flame will rise that will be seen as far as Narvik.
Risha – 8 years.

"That's it, he's all mine!"

"So it seems Risha, but that's all I managed to understand. What sand dunes? Where's Narvik?"

"Narvik sounds Scandinavian; you'll need to look it up. But I know what the sand dunes are referring to."

"What?"

"During the wedding, Jane took me aside and said she was very worried about Yune until Jawdat shared with her the news that he had been offered a very prestigious job in Kuwait. You do know Kuwait?"

"Of course, I do."

"Well, you don't know where Narvik is."

"Continue, Risha."

"So she was saying that she thought the move to Kuwait would be good for Yune because he needs to get his mind off Maryam. Of course, little does she know that by the time I'm through with him, he probably will have trouble remembering his sister's name."

"You know what? You and Nur have a lot in common."

"And why are you changing the subject?"

"I just thought I would let you know that both of you tend to be very sarcastic. Or perhaps I should be nice and say witty?"

"She may be sarcastic, but I'm definitely witty. Witty and pretty. See, it even rhymes. Pretty, witty. Witty, pretty."

"Stop."

"Then allow me to continue sharing my fascinating insight. If all goes well, they will be moving to Kuwait by the end of August."

"Will you go?"

"Will I go? I'm supposed to go, remember? For the next eight years, I'm going to haunt him. Everywhere he looks he's going to see a version of me."

"Fine Risha. I must admit, you got my mind off that wedding."

"Just sit down, relax and watch me. And don't forget to find out where Narvik is."

"Where are you going?"

"I'm leaving for Kuwait, I need to apply to the ASK."

"ASK.?"

"American School of Kuwait."

"Are you serious?"

"My dear Raqeem, what could possibly be more seductive for a ten-year-old than his beautiful librarian?"

✤

Later that day, Nur walked into my cave. She seemed truly enraged.

"I just want to say that, yes, I have full respect for the content of these scrolls, but it seems to make no sense at all that everything that I so beautifully achieved over the last two years with both Maryam and Yune is about to be entirely shattered by Risha! Why Risha?"

"You know that it's not polite to disagree with these messages, Nur."

"You seem to have forgotten that angels argued with the very creation of Adam. What is not appropriate is to keep these sentiments hidden."

"So now you have voiced them. Let's just trust that all is going to be OK."

"Going to be OK? Now you even sound like Risha! Thanks for your help."

"Wait, I need to ask you something. Would you happen to know where Narvik is?"

Nur gave me an angry look and walked out of my cave.

❖

Yune was nervous on his first day at the ASK. Too much was new: the city, the house, the weather, the school, the students, the teachers. Nothing felt right. When it was announced that his sixth and final period was free, he decided he would visit the library. Perhaps he could drown it all in a good book.

"My name is Miss Trisha. I am the librarian. This must be your first time here. May I give you a tour?"

Yune was suddenly on a different planet. There was something about this librarian that he couldn't quite understand. Wherever his eyes happened to fall on her, there was something that left him with this funny fragile feeling in his stomach. When he looked downwards, he saw the high-heeled wooden slippers. Above, was the black T-shirt which contrasted against her light brownish hair. But it was the smile that captured Yune the most. That smile that seemed to say, "Come to me. Come to me when you are being bullied; come to me when Miss Jackson, your math teacher, decides you are clearly below average; come to me when Sarah, the girl sitting next to you, turns away when you say good morning; come to me when Kuwait overwhelms you with its heat and humidity; come to me Yune and I'll be waiting here for you."

Miss Trisha had stopped at one of the shelves and seemed to be explaining to Yune something about the movie collection, but he was not listening. It was as though he was still trying to grasp the dimensions of her smile. Then suddenly, he heard her say:

"So what did you decide? Are you going to start with *Ryan's Daughter* or *The Go Between*?"

Yune reached to one of the video tapes in Miss Trisha's hand and said: "I'll borrow this one today." He said this and turned around and walked straight to the door, trying his best to keep his feet on the ground.

And so began a phase which Risha liked to call "Educating Yune." I would often show up at her home in Kuwait and ask her to explain to me exactly what she was doing with the young boy. But Risha was always capable of silencing my concerns, though a certain level of discomfort never quite left me.

"Why would you start his education with a movie about a love story between an Irish country girl and a British soldier?"

"There is so much more in *Ryan's Daughter* than a mere love story."

"Such as?"

"Such as her willingness to go against everything in the name of her love. Rosy, Ryan's daughter, goes against her people, her father, her husband and, most important, her very sense of who she is for the sake of her love. She does all this and is humiliated and almost killed in the process."

"I fail to see how this relates to Yune."

"Look, neither one of us knows what Yune is meant to carry out, but we both know that he will be met with a lot of resistance. Anyone who tries to reform anything on this planet is met with resistance."

"Yes."

"So, it's no wonder that Maryam would share with him the story of Bisher the Barefooted. Don't laugh, but *Ryan's Daughter* is just a variation to Bisher's story."

"Interesting. I'm sure Nur would find your interconnections fascinating."

"And why would you bring up Nur!?"

"Don't look at me like that."

"I'm still waiting for an answer."

"I was just trying to insert a comic touch into our conversation. Forgive me, I will not repeat it."

"Forgiven, but I still plan on tickling you."

The thought of being tickled by Risha was enough to shift my attention way beyond her choice of movies. But *Ryan's Daughter* was only the beginning. *The Go-Between, Somewhere in Time*, and many others followed. The last movie I recall she shared with him was the one I had the most trouble with: *American Gigolo*! I was so alarmed I even contemplated informing Wahi that Risha could not possibly be performing in accordance with her assigned task. Yet, once again, Risha silenced me, even made feel guilty for questioning her actions.

"Look, Yune is a teenager. He's thirteen, and like all teenage boys, he has a lot of sexual thoughts. Don't give me that look, of course, he does! So I chose a movie that has a sexual theme, yes, I did. But it's only the frame. The content, the real content, once again, is the woman who sacrifices everything, her wealth, her security and her reputation, for the man she loves. The whole movie to me and, in turn to Yune—you do know that I always have a small talk with him about the movies I share with him—the whole movie is all about that brief encounter that takes place between Julian and Michelle, the wife of an important senator, after she confesses to the police to have been with him on the night a crime took place. She did this knowing that she was throwing everything away, her entire life. I know this dialogue by heart. It takes place at the police station. They are separated by a glass barrier, and they must use handsets to speak to each other."

Julian says: "You didn't have to do that, Michelle. You could have forgotten me." And Michelle responds: "I'd rather die." Then Julian asks: "Why did you do it?" And Michelle provides that beautiful Bisher response: "I had no choice." Then she adds, "I love you." Julian hears this and, as though unable to believe that such love truly exists, he puts the phone down and whispers to himself: "My God, Michelle... it's taken me so long to come to you."

You see, it's really Bisher the Barefooted again. All the movies I share with him have a Bisher hidden within them. They all have Bisher's willingness to leave everything behind and run barefooted towards his destiny."

"Risha, you leave me speechless."

"I want to hear you repeat that in Nur's presence!"

❖

Yune was fascinated by books on philosophy and religion. Often, during the long periods of time he spent at the library, he would search for advanced works on philosophy. Frequently consulting a dictionary, he would read through these books so very carefully; it was as though he was preparing for an exam of some sorts. Risha neither encouraged this trait in Yune nor discouraged it. What was important to her was his willingness to read the books she selected for him.

Risha chose many books for Yune, mostly books of poetry and a few novels. She had him read Blake, John Donne, Lord Byron, Yeats—what was it that made her focus on the Romantics?

"Because they are spiritual and sensual at once! Very much like me!"

"Be serious, please."

"Raqeem, what I wanted Yune to experience was their vision of the journey, that beautiful journey toward one's destiny, whatever it might be. Like the Qur'anic account of the journey which Moses undertook to meet his spiritual teacher: 'I will reach that place where the two seas collide even if I must travel on for centuries.' Isn't it the same journey Blake invokes?

> *Ride ten thousand days and nights,*
> *Till age snow white hairs on thee,*
> *Thou, when thou return'st, wilt tell me,*
> *All strange wonders that befell thee,*

Or John Donne?

> *Dear child, I also by pleasant streams*
> *Have wandered all night in the Land of Dreams;*
> *But though calm and warm the waters wide,*
> *I could not get to the other side.*

Or even Lord Byron?

> *I would I were a careless child,*
> *Still dwelling in my Highland cave,*
> *Or roaming through the dusky wild,*
> *Or bounding o'er the dark blue wave;*

But no one says it more beautifully than Yeats!

> *Come away, O human child!*
> *To the waters and the wild*
> *With a faery, hand in hand,*
> *For the world's more full of weeping than you can understand."*

"Beautiful verses, when exactly did you memorize all this?"

"I have a photographic memory. Everything I read, I commit to memory, but only of course if I like what I read!"

"Very interesting. I'll make sure that this trait of yours is fully utilized. But I really don't understand why the focus on the journey?"

"Because, my dear Raqeem, when Yune is ready, his journey will begin. Remember the words of the scroll:

... a flame will rise that will be seen as far as Narvik.

"Narvik, by the way, is in northern Norway."

"I know. I know. I looked it up. What could possibly take our Yune to Narvik."

"Don't worry Miss Trisha will take care of that. Oh, and please stop doubting me."

❖

Omar Imady

2

London – June, 1980

It was in the summer of 1980 when Yune's first journey took place. He had come across an announcement at school asking students to sign up for a student trip to London. Students would be escorted by Miss Trisha, ASK's beautiful librarian and Yune's favorite person on earth at this point!

After watching *Evita*, *Les Miserables*, and *Cats*; after tours on the Thames, and visits to the Tower of London and Madame Tussaud's, after walks through Hyde Park carrying fish and chips in paper bags, then running to find cover from the sudden and frequent rain showers, after two weeks of having breakfast, lunch and dinner with Miss Trisha, after all of this, Yune and two of his friends, Adib and Sameer, were allowed to experience London at night without Miss Trisha's supervision. Yes, they had to return by eleven and had a long list of instructions on what they should and shouldn't do. Nevertheless, this was their night to explore and conquer.

They first walked around Piccadilly Circus. They had been there before, but they wanted to experience it without Miss Trisha's watchful eyes. When they started getting hungry, they took the underground to Oxford Circus where they'd been told lots of good restaurants were located. But they talked and talked and got distracted and, by the time they noticed, they had passed their destination. They got off at Maida Vale, a small and fairly old station. It felt like centuries before their trip up the steep escalator was over. As they walked out of the station, they noticed to their left a Japanese restaurant named Chosan.

Inside, the place looked like a Japanese tea house. A waitress in her late twenties wearing a kimono and white socks greeted them and asked them to take off their shoes. Once they had complied, she guided them to one of the small tables near the window. They smiled as they sat on the traditional *tatami* mats. Moments later she came back with the menus, and as she handed one to Yune, her left hand took hold of his shoulder and squeezed it slightly. Flustered and surprised, Yune turned his head to her and found her smiling, but it was not the smile of someone who had just done something by mistake nor the smile of an adult trying to make someone much younger comfortable. No, it was the smile of a woman who had just made a serious pass and who felt absolutely no remorse! Yune's friends didn't notice what had taken place, and Yune decided to ignore it. But later when their food arrived, she placed her hand on the back of his neck and her fingers gently caressed his hair. When he looked at her this time, she asked if he was enjoying his food. Yune, who had not even had the chance to taste his food yet, blushed and nodded his head. But his friends had now noticed this strange show of affection, and Yune had to listen to their sharp comments.

"We didn't know about your Japanese connections!"

"What is it about you that attracts waitresses?"

Yune ate fast and hoped it would all be over quickly, but more, much more was still to come.

"What type of dessert would you like?" the waitress asked Yune, ignoring the presence of his friends. When Yune gestured that he was full and could eat no more, she said: "Then you must try our tea, it's green tea with jasmine, known for its healing qualities." "Yes," Adib, added, "it has very strong healing qualities." It was then that Yune asked firmly for the bill and in a few moments, was heading towards to the door. He put his shoes on, stepped out and waited for his friends to follow. The first one out, however, was the waitress. She rushed toward him as though he was her long lost lover. Yune, ironically, seemed more intrigued by her feet. The thought that she had not even bothered to put slippers or shoes on before leaving the restaurant, this seemingly insignificant detail, seemed to have captivated him so much that when she took hold of his arm and started walking with him, he showed no resistance at all. His friends caught up with them and asked what on earth was going on? Yune asked them to return alone. He promised he would soon follow. They reminded him of Miss Trisha and pointed out that he was violating all of her instructions. He repeated his request to be left alone and walked away with …?

"What is your name?"

"What would you like it to be?"

"Rosy. Tonight you are my Rosy. Have you heard of *Ryan's Daughter* by any chance?"

I wondered if I should just stop watching and travel to London. I wanted to ask Risha if she knew where Yune was tonight. Who he was with? And what apparently he's about to engage in? But the thought of being told that I failed to trust her again kept me from acting upon my impulse.

They took the underground to Marble Arch and, from there they took the 159 bus to Streatham, a suburb of south London, where Risha and her ASK students were staying. Along the way, they were mostly silent. Whenever Yune looked at her, she would say, "After all this time, we meet again." Yune would just smile and shake his head. Something in him must have thought she was mad, but most of his attention was still captivated by the feet in white socks.

They got off near Streatham Common, a large park only a few minutes away from the house he was staying at, but

Yune was clearly not heading towards the house. They walked directly towards the park. The grass was damp. Rosy abandoned her socks. Yune looked back; was he wondering if she was deliberately leaving evidence behind? Yune looked down; was he wondering how the dampness felt against her bare feet? They reached a small hill with two large oak trees. Why did they want a secluded place? Yune just stared as Rosy began to take off his shirt. Gently and slowly she began to kiss him, first on the forehead, next on his nose, and finally on his lips. It seemed as though it lasted forever. Regardless of how Risha was going to react, I was determined to arrive at Streatham Common in a manner of seconds, disguised for the very first time since my arrival on earth as a ruthless mugger! All that was necessary was for that kiss to evolve into the inevitable next step. But Yune turned out to be a master of surprises! He moved his head away from hers. He actually moved away, tilted his head downwards, stood up, whispered something into her ear, and walked away. She didn't follow him. Was she expecting him to return?

Yune walked quickly to the house. He found Adib sitting on the door steps. "Where on earth have you been? It's nearly midnight!" Yune ignored him, walked in and climbed the stairs to Risha's room. He didn't knock. She was sitting on the bed and staring out of the open window when he walked in. He rushed to her, threw his head on her lap and cried. She placed her hand on his eyes and said, "Hush, my child. Hush. It's all going to be beautiful, I promise."

❖

Narvik - July, 1983

In the summer of '83, Yune embarked on a trip to Narvik, a town located in northern Norway, around 220 km north of the Arctic Circle. Risha first introduced the idea to Yune when she shared with him a book entitled *Norway, Land of the Midnight Sun*. Shortly after, she had him watch *The Man Who Would Be King*, a movie about a voyage which two men undertake to Kafiristan, an exotic province of northeast Afghanistan now known as Nuristan. Still, Yune did not seem moved. Then Risha decided she would introduce him to Maya, an ASK student with a Syrian father and a Norwegian mother. The challenge was not so much arranging a setting within which they would interact since the library was of course an ideal location, but rather it was ensuring that some type of positive chemical interaction would take place between them. Maya was shy and reserved. She had never had a boyfriend and didn't seem like she was at all interested in the idea. Yune, on other hand, was interested in only one woman: Risha. She was not only the heir of Maryam's aesthetic and spiritual voice, but she was also the object of Yune's teenage desires and fantasies.

Risha decided she had to rely on Maya. After all, Maya's lack of interest in boys seemed easier to conquer than Yune's overwhelming interest with his librarian. And so Risha undertook a borderline violation of guidelines pertaining to the type of behavior we can induce in humans. Yes, Risha pulled Maya into an electrifying infatuation with Yune.

On a February afternoon, I watched as Maya walked slowly to where Yune was sitting in the library. Her dark brown eyes were clearly her father's, but her height and hair color were distinctly Norwegian. She smiled and sat down. Yune was reading a book entitled: *The Oneness of God - Implications on Thought and Life*. He stared at her for a few seconds. Like all ASK female students, she had on a dark blue skirt and a white shirt. Her hair was braided into a bun in the back.

"Miss Trisha told me you are interested in Norway."

"She did?"

"Yes. I would love to talk to you about Norway. My mom is from Oslo, the capital of Norway."

"Yes, I know."

"You do?"

"Well, I know it's the capital, but I didn't know your mom was from there."

"That's funny."

Maya giggled as her hand reached to Yune in a seemingly innocent show of affection. Yune seemed confused. He didn't expect that the touch of her hand over his would feel so sweet, so warm. He wanted to react, to say something:

"So when do we start talking about Norway?"

In the months that followed this encounter, Yune came to enjoy and cherish the time he spent with Maya. His first experiments in writing poetry were inspired by his desire to share thoughts and feelings with her. At times he would even share the same poem with Maya and Risha. But Risha was careful not to make him feel any type of disloyalty or inner conflict. What Risha was primarily interested in was ensuring that whatever was taking place between Yune and Maya would eventually become the foundation for a trip to the land of the midnight sun.

Though Maya's father was liberal in many ways, the idea of his daughter meeting Yune on a regular basis was not one that he could easily tolerate. But Maya had a brother, Basel, whom Yune quickly befriended. Basel became the perfect excuse for Yune's frequent visits to Maya's home. Often during such visits, the time Yune could spend with Maya was very short. Even when her father wasn't home, both her mother and older sister would insist on keeping Yune's visits exactly what they pretended to be, visits to Basel. Only on rare occasions, would they meet alone at the very top of her apartment building's stairs. They would sit on the floor near the locked door of the building's roof holding hands and wondering if someone had noticed them climb the stairs, and if someone would notice them climb down.

It was during those long passages of time in Basel's room, waiting for Maya to find yet another excuse to pass by her brother's room, if only for a few moments, that the thorough planning for a trip to the land of the midnight sun was undertaken. Narvik was actually proposed by Maya's mom when she found out they were interested in visiting northern Norway. Yune, recalling the various stories he had heard about Narvik from Risha, embraced the idea enthusiastically.

Maya and her family would leave for Oslo on their annual vacation in late June, and Yune would follow in mid July. He would spend a few days in Oslo, and then they would buy U-rail train tickets that would allow them to travel anywhere in Scandinavia for two weeks. They had to reach Narvik before the 18th of July, the last day the sun is above the horizon.

One day prior to his departure to Oslo, Yune met Risha at the library.

"I'm leaving tomorrow."

"Tomorrow?"

"Tomorrow."

"All the way to Narvik?"

"Yes."

"I want you to promise me something."

"Yes, anything."

"Open your hand."

Yune opened his hand and stared at her in anticipation. She placed a small bright yellow envelope in his hand and said:

"When you see the midnight sun, I want you to open this and recite the words it contains."

Yune nodded his head and walked towards the library's main entrance. He stood there for a few seconds as though to soak her image into his eyes and then walked out.

❖

It was a Saturday morning, the 16th of July, when Basel and Yune got on a train heading from Oslo to Trondheim. They arrived around seven hours later. Then, they took another train to Storlien on the Swedish border. Narvik couldn't be reached directly from Trondheim, and they, in fact, had to travel east to Sweden and then northwest to Narvik. From Storlien, they traveled to Ãnge and then to Boden, which they reached after more than twenty-one hours of traveling. They were exhausted, hungry and, most important, unable to visualize themselves getting on yet another train! Though they were only six hours away from Narvik, Basel was adamant that they should sleep at Boden and then take a train south to Stockholm. Narvik and its midnight sun would be abandoned!

"Listen, Yune, I have had enough with all this nature. It's cool, OK. But I want civilization. I want a modern Scandinavian city now!"

"And the midnight sun?"

"Can we please forget the midnight sun? I just can't hear about it anymore. Look, it was still sunny last night at around eleven o'clock. So what possible difference is it going to make to experience sunlight at midnight?"

"It's not that; it's the sight of the sun setting above the horizon."

"Man, that's only if it's not cloudy. Everyone we talked to said it's almost always cloudy."

Yune hesitated. Thoughts of a real bed in Boden and, later, of a good restaurant in a city like Stockholm seemed to dance in his mind. But just when I was wondering if Risha's elaborate plan was about to crumble, a young woman appeared in a bright yellow dress. She walked on the platform as though performing on a catwalk. As Yune stared at her, his hand, almost by reflex, reached to his pocket where he had placed Risha's small envelope. He peeked at it and then shoved it back in. The woman in the yellow dress was now standing right in front of Basel and him.

"Excuse me, but do you know when the train to Narvik will arrive?"

Her question was directed at both of them, but she was only looking at Yune.

Yune answered:

"It will arrive in around half an hour, forty minutes to be exact."

"Thank you. Are you going to Narvik too by any chance?"

Yune didn't hesitate:

"Yes, of course. Narvik is my destination."

Basel's mouth opened in complete disbelief and utter contempt.

"Well, I wish you both a very safe trip to Narvik." Basel said this and walked out of the station.

Yune and Anna, as her name turned out to be, sat next to each other and shared stories about their lives and dreams. He told her how much she reminded him of a woman who was much more than a librarian, and she told him about all the beauty she expected to see at Narvik. But somewhere along the way, Yune fell asleep, and when he finally woke up at Narvik station, Anna had disappeared.

It was Sunday, the 17th of July at around two in the afternoon when Yune checked into a small hotel in Narvik. There, he took a hot shower and then relished in his capacity to lie down on a comfortable bed. He thought about Basel and what he might be doing in Boden, about Maya in her Oslo home, and about Miss Trisha amidst her books and movies. Around ten, Yune left his room. He asked a man at the reception desk where the best spot to see the midnight sun was.

"Well, actually, anywhere would be great tonight. The sky is so clear. Take the cable car to the top of the mountain.

It's very close to the hotel. You will have a beautiful view of the midnight sun."

And so on the night of the 17th of July, Yune stood on Mount Fagernesfjellet overlooking Narvik. Moments before midnight, as the sun reached its lowest point above the horizon, he opened Risha's yellow envelope. Inside it, to his dismay, was a poem he had once written and shared with both Maya and Risha:

> *A few minutes before sunset*
> *An angel arrives*
> *To collect a world*
> *That danced beneath the sun.*
> *Your mind danced for rain*
> *Your heart, for a window.*
> *Your body, for a frame.*
> *But a voice whispered from a distance:*
> *May the fragments soon become one.*

❖

I've often wondered why Yune had to go to Narvik. Why send a seventeen-year-old to the Arctic Circle? What was it that he was supposed to learn through such a journey? Had he met someone there, someone like the spiritual guide Moses met at the point where the two seas collided, it would have all made sense. 'Travel even to Narvik in search of a spiritual guide' would have been the secret of such a journey. But Yune meets no one. When he arrives, Risha has him recite one of his own poems!

I shared my confusion with Risha. In retrospect, maybe I shouldn't have.

"So why was Yune sent to Narvik?"

"I can't believe you would ask this question. I thought we both understood this so clearly!"

"You're patronizing me."

"I love to patronize you."

"So it appears you don't have any idea either."

"Of course I do. If I didn't experience the message I couldn't help unfold it. Yune had to go to Narvik, had to stand alone in Narvik, and had to recite his own words in Narvik; he had to do all this to learn a very important lesson!"

"What? What lesson?"

"That sometimes in life, you may have to cross a very long distance and the only person you will meet at your final destination is yourself, the only voice you will hear is your own."

"You must be kidding. Why would Yune have to learn such a lesson?"

"Now you're departing my domain. To answer your question, I would have to know what Yune's ultimate purpose is, for what exactly he is being prepared. Do you know the answer to these questions?"

"You know I don't."

"Well, sometimes I wonder...Just kidding."

✣

During his senior year at ASK, Yune showed himself to have fully internalized his librarian's methods. He had so perfected the art of seduction that he was by far the most popular young man at ASK. With his black T-shirt, jeans and boots, with his long ash blond hair and slender, almost feminine build, and, most important, with a personality that was a cross between John Donne's sensuality and Blake's spirituality, Yune left many girls his age thirsty for some type of contact with him. Though Miss Trisha remained very special to Yune, his visits to her towards the end of his senior year were prompted by his desire to share his latest experiences rather than by his desire to learn or become inspired. His education was clearly completed.

✛

3

Encouraged by Robert, his maternal cousin, Yune applied to Macalester College in St. Paul Minnesota. He applied to no other place and by May, he had received his acceptance letter. He was to depart Kuwait in July. I confess to have been very concerned. Yune appeared to be so totally uninhibited that the thought of him traveling to St. Paul and attending wild freshmen parties at Macalester made me wish the five months that were left before scroll two of the third cylinder could be opened were over tomorrow. I carried my concerns to Risha one evening.

"What exactly are the red lines? What exactly is Yune not allowed to do?"

"You're asking me, the angel of seduction about lines? Red lines?"

"Whom else do I ask Risha? You're his guardian angel for yet another five months."

"You sound like you would rather it were not the case!"

"I'm just concerned, Risha. Aren't you? If he were to encounter a young woman in a park again who is as willing and eager as that Japanese waitress once was, would he rush into your arms again? I sincerely doubt it. He has none of the inhibitions of the past."

"It's remarkable that I need to put you, the angel responsible for weaving contradictory paths into a purposeful plot, on the right wave length! How could you possibly assume that Yune's inhibitions are responsible for protecting him from violating these things you call red lines? Even when you take everything we help facilitate into consideration, there is still much more going on. What I'm trying to say is ..."

"That it simply can't go wrong?"

"Yes, Raqeem. And not because we are so brilliant at what we do."

"Because in addition to us, the design has its own hidden agents that intervene when we can't?"

"Or perhaps it's simply Yune's ultimate purpose that cannot be violated even if Yune himself tried his very best to do so. Remember Jonah?"

"Yune's namesake?"

"Yes, the Yunus of the Bible and the Qur'an. He tries to escape his purpose and finds himself in a whale, only to be cast on the shore to fulfill what his ultimate purpose was all along, inviting his city to monotheism!"

"In other words, your very attempt to escape the design is part of the design?"

"Beautifully put, Raqeem! Now if I don't stop speaking like this, I'm going to start feeling like I'm someone else. I kind of do already actually, and I'm not sure I like the feeling."

"Nur?"

"Yes. Yes. So enough of Nur, please. Just have faith, my dear Raqeem and stop worrying about lines, red or otherwise!"

❖

In July, Yune said goodbye to Kuwait. His last encounter with Maya was very sweet. He arrived at her home moments after her father had left to work. She was wearing flannel pink pajamas. As her mom made breakfast in the kitchen, they stood at the door and exchanged a few words. He held her hand as though to say, "Thank you. I'm so sorry I couldn't love you in the beautiful way you loved me."

The Gospel of Damascus

His farewell to Risha was more intense. He left the library only after he had made her promise to write him on a weekly basis, to phone him at least once a month and to do all she could to visit St. Paul. Then he even gathered all his courage and kissed her on the cheek, a long kiss that expressed eight years of gratitude and, yes, that made me a bit jealous. Little did he know that Risha had already planned her reemergence in St. Paul, this time as one of the caretakers of Dupre Hall.

❖

Yune planned his trip to St Paul as meticulously as Basel and he had once planned their trip to northern Scandinavia. The more he traveled by cars, trains and boats, the less he seemed to like the idea of flying. He left Kuwait by car to Damascus with one of his father's friends. From Damascus he took a bus to Tartus, a Syrian port city on the Mediterranean where he embarked on a Russian cargo ship that was heading to, Limassol, Cyprus. There, he met Hadi, a friend from Kuwait who had arrived by plane earlier. After staying a few days in a hotel predominately occupied by Asian prostitutes, Hadi's choice, they traveled by boat to Venice. Twenty-four hours later, they were in the city of love and romance. A week later, they took a train to Rome where they played with my nerves for around two weeks! In early August, Yune finally said goodbye to Hadi and took a train all the way to Southampton. This was, of course, before the Chunnel, and so there was a channel crossing by ferry, a stop in London and then, finally, a train ride to Southampton. Why Southampton? Because on the 5th of August, Yune was to board the QE2 for a stylish six-day crossing of the Atlantic. Yune's mother, grandmother, aunt and cousin were waiting for him at the New York harbor. After a few days at Jane's ancestral home in New Rochelle, NY, Yune and his mom traveled on an Amtrak train first to Evanston where Jane's sister, Robert's mother, lived and finally to St. Paul, arriving there on the 26th of August, 1984.

Of all the times I worried about Yune during his long journey to St. Paul, yes, despite Risha's comforting words, none competed with the time he spent in Rome. It was there that Yune met Beatris, a Swiss young woman traveling through Italy. In a sense it could all be blamed on feet! Yes, feet. Female feet in particular, caressing the water of the Fountain of the Naiads at the Piazza della Republica. Yune had left Hadi enjoying his espresso at a nearby café to get a closer look at the fountain. Awaiting him were four nymphs once sculpted by Mario Rutelli and a fifth enjoying a foot bath with her skirt pulled way above her knees. Her skin was creamy white with a hint of rose. I've always known Yune had some type of foot fetish. I watched him carefully as he observed his librarian's feet for hours. And Risha, no doubt, played on this and changed her sandals, slippers, and clogs on a daily basis. But I don't recall ever seeing him so captivated. Did the presence of Rutelli's nymphs fill the air with sensuality or was it simply this woman's feet playing with the water, or both? Then he approached her.

"What you are doing can be very dangerous."

"Dangerous? Why, is it the water?" she replied with a distinct German accent.

"No. It's the eyes."

"The eyes? Whose eyes?"

"Mine."

"I'm sorry, but I don't understand."

"If your beautiful feet keep pressing against each other in the water, I might have to ask you to have some lemon gelato with me."

She hesitated, then blushed, then smiled, then nodded her head.

The Gospel of Damascus

In a few minutes, Hadi had been forgotten, and they were both at an ice cream shop having a very lemony Italian version of ice cream. But if it was Yune who initiated this event, this young woman with short golden curly hair was quickly to take over.

"There is something very sexy about lemons, yeah?"

"Yeah."

"You want to taste mine?"

"I think mine is quite similar to yours, but sure."

Yune expected her spoon to approach his lips. Instead it was her mouth full of lemon ice cream and in a fraction of a second; he was being kissed like he never had been before. His eyes stayed open as though to express how perplexed he was at the combination of sensations that he was experiencing. When the conversation shifted toward where she was staying, how close her hotel happened to be, and how much she would like to show him the view from her window, I just had to do something, something I could never confess to Risha.

"Where have you been?" asked Hadi, clearly disturbed and unamused by the sight of Beatris who by now was sitting on Yune's lap.

"How did you find me?"

"Well, if it wasn't for Alberto, I would never have guessed you were here."

"Alberto? Who's Alberto?"

"You're asking me? You're the one who sent him. Can we please leave? Good to meet you ..."

"Beatris."

"Yes, Beatris, I'm very sorry, but we really need to go now."

Hadi said this, as he practically dragged Yune out of his chair.

❖

Omar Imady

St. Paul – Fall, 1984

Yune and his mom arrived in St. Paul in late August. They walked into Macalester College with a large black trunk. Jane had done her homework and consulted many of her friends and the friends of her friends and their unanimous advice was that a trunk had to be purchased, along with a down jacket, water-proof boots, thermal underwear and lots and lots of sweaters. But St. Paul in August was hot and humid. Yune chose not to argue with his mother about the exact function of this black trunk or its contents. He was too eager to immerse himself in college life. He hugged her and thanked her for all that she had done.

"Take this. It has a few phone numbers you might need."

Yune took a quick glance at the paper.

"The Islamic Center?"

"Yes, I found out there's one in Columbia Heights, not too far from here."

"Thank you Mom. Please let me know when you return safely. Love you."

Yune left his mom at the Student Union to finish her coffee. A taxi was soon to pick her up and drive her to the airport. He walked toward Dupre Hall dragging his heavy black trunk and wondering why on earth he would ever want to contact an Islamic Center here in Minnesota, when even in Kuwait, he rarely went to Friday prayer with his father? Little did he know that in less than five months, he would drive toward Columbia Heights during a heavy snow storm in search of that very Islamic Center!

❖

"My name is Debra Koch, welcome to West Dupre. Your room is 201. You'll be sharing it with Chris. He's a really friendly guy from New Jersey."

78

"There is something about Debra," I could almost hear Yune wondering. He waited until she had left the room and then opened the trunk and started to empty its contents. Suddenly, the sound of Elvis Costello singing "You better watch your step" filled the room. Chris had entered the room and instantaneously enacted his ritual of entry, pressing the playback button on his Sony recorder.

"Hey, I'm Chris. I see you had to get a black trunk, too?"

"Sure did. I'm Yune."

"Yune?"

"That's right. It's Arabic for Jonah."

"Sounds cool. Listen, take a shower and get dressed, Mr. Yune. We have a lot of parties to visit tonight. I'll be your special guide. Oh, by the way, I hope you like Elvis Costello?"

"Love him." Yune had in fact never heard of Costello!

"Good, because I listen to him all the time, all the time!"

And so, with Chris leading the way, Yune visited countless dorm parties. Until mid-September when classes were to begin, Yune spent most of his time with Chris, and at times they even slept right next to each other in the hallways of Macalester's dorms.

"Hey, that's your head on my shoulder!"

"Sorry, man. Where exactly are we?"

"Somewhere in Wallace."

"How did we get to Wallace? Weren't we in Bigelow?"

"Bigelow? We've never set foot in Bigelow!"

"You may be in Wallace, man, but I'm definitely in Bigelow!"

❖

Once, during a party that was held at Turck Hall, Yune, feeling a sudden need for fresh air, decided to go outside for a few minutes. As he was heading to the main door, someone called out for him.

"Hey, Yune, it's me. Walid."

Walid was a Kuwaiti student whom Yune met in a party held at the International Center. Though they didn't know each other in Kuwait, Walid loved the idea of meeting someone in St. Paul who once lived in his country.

"Come on in, this is my room. Have a seat. Something to drink?"

"No, thanks, just some air. Would you mind opening the window?"

Just then, a girl walked in. She was around 5'5", with distinctly wide shoulders. Her hair was short, dark red and permed. She was wearing pajamas, navy pajamas which contrasted beautifully with her pale complexion. But most striking of all was the fact that she was barefooted! Yune said nothing, even as Walid tried to introduce them. He was so captivated by the energy she carried with her into the room that he didn't even hear Walid speaking.

"He is not always this impolite, Amanda. He does talk sometimes. Hey man, look at me. This is Amanda. Her room is right across from mine."

"I'm sorry. I'm still a bit dazed from the party I was at. My name is Yune."

"Yune? Is that Swiss?"

"No, you must be thinking of Carl Jung?"

"That's right."

"Yes, but my name is just Yune with an e. It's the Arabic version of Jonah."

"I'm curious. I would like to hear more about this. Where are you from?"

"Well, that's actually complicated. You might say Damascus."

"Damascus? You don't look like you're from Damascus."

"You see, that's why it's complicated."

"I love complicated. You want to have a walk and just talk."

"Yes. Let's do that."

And so he walked along with Amanda in her navy pajamas and bare feet. They walked down Grand Avenue all the way to RC Dick's Market and back. He talked and talked like he never had before. No one he had previously met was interested in his views on religion, politics, and life in general. There was nothing Amanda didn't enjoy talking about with an amazing combination of both tolerance and passion. When he finally walked her back to her room, there was none of that awkward feeling in the air, none of that who will kiss whom first and whether or not he or she should invite the other in. This time, it was simply, "That was a great talk. We've got to continue this tomorrow." Yune looked down and took one final look at her feet and headed back to Dupre.

Back at his room, he found Chris caressing the hair of a cute brunette.

"Hey, Yune. Where have you been?"

"Just walking."

"This is Anneke, from Holland."

"Hello Anneke. Should I come back later?"

"No, no. Please stay. I was just telling her about that great exotic stuff with olive oil."

The "exotic stuff with olive oil" was *za'tar* or thyme and sesame seeds, as popular in Syria as peanut butter is in the States. Yune prepared a small bowl and handed it to them with a bag of crackers. He felt unusually peaceful this evening. He lay on his bed and quickly fell asleep as Chris and Anneke kissed and Costello sang "Man out of Time."

❖

In the days that followed, Yune and Amanda met often. He learned that she was from St. Paul and that her parents were divorced. She was raised by her mom but looked, and often acted, a lot like her father. She described herself as a liberal democrat, a disillusioned Christian and above all, a feminist. In her room it wasn't Costello who was always on, but rather the more sophisticated piano albums of George Winston.

Yune's relationship with Amanda comforted me like nothing had in Yune's life since Maryam. Ironically, Risha, now disguised as Debra Koch, didn't like Amanda at all. I lost count of how many times she tried to interrupt their conversations when they took place in Yune's room. And so I decided in early October to visit Risha in West Dupre.

"My dear Raqeem, or should I say Alberto."

"You saw that?"

"You're not the only one with screens you know! You were true to your heart, but you should feel sorry for Beatris. You really scared her!"

"Forget Beatris. What's your problem with Amanda?"

"Amanda. Amanda. I don't like her. It's true."

"Why?"

"Look, I know my time with Yune is about to be completed. And I know I have nothing left to teach him. But even if there is one day left, I will not let anyone blow out the flame I have done so much to kindle. Not Amanda, not anyone."

"But why do you think Amanda would do that?"

"Well, the very fact that she comforts you is enough proof that she cannot be trusted with my flame. Capisce, Alberto?"

"Understood. I just have one more question, who exactly is Debra Koch?"

"Debra is the girl who was supposed to arrive this fall to be this floor's caretaker! Unfortunately, she had some difficulty arriving this semester. You've heard of mono, it's very common in the Midwest."

"Interesting! What's going to happen when they find out you were falsifying your identity?"

"They can look for me at Mount Hermon!"

My visit was clearly a failure. Risha actually became more assertive in her anti-Amanda tactics. She identified an American version of Maya and introduced her to Yune. Lily was a beautiful blonde who lived one floor above Amanda in Turck. In so many ways she was the antithesis of Amanda. She followed Yune everywhere and she wasn't at all interested in any intellectual discussions. She was content to just be around him. Yune didn't mind the attention, especially since Lily never pushed sexual intimacy though she did frequently hold his hand and kiss him. But eventually, and to Risha's detriment, the time he spent with Amanda left little, if any, time to spend with Lily.

Only once did Yune seem vulnerable to Lily. He was near her room one evening and so he decided he would drop by and say hello. The door wasn't locked as usual, and when he entered he found her standing in front of a mirror wearing only a red towel. She had just come out of the shower and her hair was still wet. She walked toward him and without saying a word, turned off the lights. Then she led him to her bed and gestured for him to sit. He complied. She dropped the towel and began to get dressed. A short turquoise dress with nothing underneath. Then thigh-high stockings, white and sheer, followed. She sprayed some perfume on her neck from a bottle of CK and then sat very close to him. What transpired in the next few minutes, or more specifically the way in which Yune experienced it, was later recorded by Yune in a poem:

The moments you paused to draw a circle or
erect a flag
betrayed your seductive design.
You had no intention to stop.
Heat, moisture, depth were your destination.
Even time was woven into your intricate plan.
In one minute you would reach her knee.
Seconds later you would cross that line:
Separating nylon from flesh.
Innocence from eroticism.
Stratagem from conquest.
Nothing prepared you for that abrupt col-
lapse.
The avalanche of her hand over yours.
How long can you live suspended,
Barred, yet invited?

Lily's reaction was so unexpected that Yune quickly withdrew his hand and left the room. Why Lily chose to stop him from advancing further remains a mystery to both her and Yune. Later, she would put herself to sleep dreaming she had acted differently. But I do confess to having pulled her at that very instant into placing her hand firmly over Yune's. Perhaps had I not, Yune himself would have stopped on his own. But unlike Risha, processing these events was always difficult for me regardless of how convinced I was that nothing can go wrong.

It was, of course, a completely different experience to watch Yune and Amanda visit art museums, have Turkish coffee and baklava at Java restaurant in downtown Minneapolis or walk at sunset to the Mississippi river near St. Thomas. I loved to listen to them explore their intellectual horizons. And it wasn't all just talk. They translated their shared convictions into rules and even identified the exceptions to these rules. When they agreed one day that eating meat required suspending the thought of how the animal was once slaughtered, they immediately decided to become vegetarians. Fish, however, was permitted. And when Amanda shared a story of how her floor mate was nearly hospitalized because of how much alcohol she drank, they both decided to stop drinking alcoholic drinks. This didn't, however, apply to cocktails since, first, they were delicious and, second, they were only consumed at very special occasions.

Toward the end of the fall semester, Yune was asked by his aunt to spend Christmas with her in New Rochelle. Yune in turn asked Amanda if she would come along. He was to leave before Christmas, and Amanda would follow after spending Christmas day with her family. Still, Risha didn't give up. In the few days Yune was at New Rochelle before Amanda's arrival when he was mostly going out with his cousin Lisa and her friends, Risha managed to pull one of them into an intense attraction to Yune which carried her straight into his bed.

"How did you arrive here? Where exactly is my cousin? What did you do to Lisa?"

"Nothing! She's asleep. Everyone is asleep. It's just me and you."

"You and me?" Yune repeated her words as he noticed that she was wearing pink cotton shorts and a sleeveless white T-shirt!

"Yes," she answered as she began to kiss him.

"There's something I must share with you."

"You're as attracted to me as I am to you?"

"Well actually, the truth is I'm gay."

She froze, withdrew her body, and without saying a word, left the room.

❖

Omar Imady

4

Amanda arrived on Friday, the 28th of December. The intellectual chemistry that characterized them was clear to everyone. Regardless of where they were and who was around them, Yune and Amanda were constantly talking. I'm sure Risha often wondered why they never seemed to run out of topics to discuss. In addition to their love of dialogue, Yune and Amanda had another thing in common; they loved fancy things, fancy restaurants and hotels in particular. So, they planned to spend New Year's Eve in New York. They put together whatever savings they had, more Yune than Amanda, and paid $225 at the Waldorf Astoria for a beautiful room overlooking Manhattan. The room, however, was not associated with physical intimacy. After watching the Ball fall and having a very classy dinner, they needed a place to rest, a fancy place to rest, that's all.

I recall that night clearly. Amanda wore a dress given to her by her grandmother. It was red, velvet, close-fitting, with matching buttons that ran from top to bottom. Around an hour after midnight, an exhausted Amanda and Yune sat at a piano bar to have a piña colada after having had to fight their way out of the endless crowds which drowned Time Square with their euphoria. It was around then that I felt the need to open the box again. Eight years were over and the second scroll of the third cylinder was ready to be opened:

His journey to Damascus will begin on this night, when the ice castle will melt beneath an eastern light.
Nur – 2 years.

"Nur, you need to leave for New York City."

"On New Year's Eve? Do you have any idea how dark and heavy the atmosphere must be."

"You've been summoned Nur. Take a look at this scroll."

"After eight years of Risha, I must now come back again?"

"Yes, you must."

"What possible sense does this make?"

"Well, there are a lot of parallels."

"Like what?"

"Last time you arrived, you did something to Yune through Maryam. This time it's going to be through Amanda."

"Amanda is the ice castle?"

"Yes, she is. A daughter of Minnesota, the land of ice castles!"

"And she brings him back to Damascus."

"Yes, but who knows when? Let's focus on tonight. They're at a piano bar right now."

"How conducive to spiritual change!"

"We agreed to stop the sarcasm."

"Fine, fine. I'll leave in a few minutes."

"Whom will you arrive as?"

"At a piano bar, what can I arrive as other than a waitress? But I guarantee you I will be very different than the waitress he once met in London."

"I have no doubt Nur."

Nur walked out of my cave, and in a few minutes she was walking around Carmen's Piano Bar wearing a white shirt and a black skirt. In place of the scarf I've never seen her without, she had on a white satin bandana.

✥

"Can I get you another drink?"

"Sure, perhaps some more piña colada?"

"Or our specialty?"

"What is it?"

"Arabian Crescent."

"What exactly is that?" Amanda asked very much intrigued.

"I'll get you some and you'll find out."

Maybe it was something she placed in the drinks or maybe it was Nur's mere presence, but it was shortly after their drinks arrived that they started talking about religion, Islam in particular.

"How come you never speak to me about Islam, you are a Muslim, aren't you?"

"Yes and no."

"Tell me about the yes."

"Well, yes, because Islam was planted in me at a very young age by someone very close to my heart."

"Who?"

"Maryam, my sister. She had this amazing faith in God."

"Tell me about her God."

"She had this vision of God that I'm very much at peace with."

"Tell me."

"God in Islam, has three attributes."

"You sound very professorial."

"Must be the Arabian Crescent! Anyway, the first is transcendence. God is not part of space and time. Nor can God be compared to anything we are familiar with. So, if you speak of God as father or son or if you use any type of similar terminology, even when it's only being used metaphorically, you are falling into the trap of describing God on our own terms."

"What's wrong with that?"

"Well, what about the daughter who was abused by her father, is it fair to ask her to relate to God as father? And then when you start describing God as a European looking man …"

"Now you're attacking my religion!"

"Wait, I thought you were disillusioned with Christianity."

"I am. But it's one thing for me to say that and it's entirely different for you to criticize the religion I grew up with."

"Amanda. I am not at all attacking Christianity. There is so much about Christianity that I am very attached to. My mom's family you know is entirely Christian. I was simply trying to explain Islam's view of God because you asked me to. Let's just drop the subject and talk about why people get so excited about the beginning of a new year?"

"Nope, I want you to continue what you were saying."

"Do you realize how defensive you've become?"

"Yes I do. Still, you can't stop now."

"Very interesting Amanda. What exactly is in your glass?"

"Nothing! It's empty, and I actually would like some more."

Nur took her order and returned quickly with another drink. It was beautiful to watch how Nur was dealing with the bartender, the waitresses and even the manager. I have on very few occasions practiced *ighsha'* or suspending people's ability to question your presence amongst them, but only for very short periods of time. It's an act that requires intense spiritual energy and I recall feeling exhausted after the few times I resorted to it.

As Nur placed the second glass of Arabian Crescent on the table, she came close to Amanda and whispered something in her ear. Amanda smiled, and for the first time in Yune's presence she blushed.

"What did she say to you?"

"Nothing you need to know. Please continue before I get even more defensive."

"Fine. As I was saying, to portray God as a European looking young man, as Christ is frequently portrayed in the West, is to place a mask on God that could possibly alienate millions of people who simply can't relate to it. What about Africans and Asians? Are they to somehow believe that God chose a Caucasian son over and above other races?"

"So which mask does Islam propose?"

"That's the point Amanda that I've been trying to make. No mask whatsoever!"

"No mask?"

"No mask. The moment you place a mask, you violate transcendence."

"OK, move on."

"What do you think this is? A McDonald's take-out?"

"I don't think this is how you should be speaking to a woman who is drinking her second Arabian Crescent!!"

"I don't think I've ever seen you in this mood."

"Well, if you want me to get out of it, continue."

"The second attribute is oneness. Maybe I should have mentioned this first. In Arabic, the word used is *tawhid*. It's even stronger than oneness, unitary works a bit better. Any implication that there is anything divine or godlike other than the One God or that this oneness can be somehow divided or distributed is rejected. It's basically an uncompromising version of monotheism."

"You're being professorial again."

"You are making it so difficult to talk and yet so difficult to stop."

"Exactly. I want to fluster you."

"Why would you do that to someone as nice as me?"

"The truth?"

"Yes, of course, the truth."

"Because you are challenging me and for the first time since we started having our talks, I don't know how to respond to you! I don't want to defend the vision of God I grew up with because, as a feminist, I have always had difficulty with its masculine layers. With the few words you have shared so far, you have unraveled the very essence of how I have approached God until tonight. Now, if you're smart, you will act like you didn't even hear me say this and just continue talking."

"OK, the third attribute is closeness or immanence. It's my favorite."

"Who exactly taught you how to speak like this?"

"I'm very well read, Amanda. For a long time, I practically lived at my high school library."

"So it appears. Continue please."

"Immanence is about God being so close, closer to us than our own hearts. This is where Islam and Christianity meet. So there you have it, let's move on to something else."

"OK. I hope that wasn't too difficult. I must admit you're very attractive when you speak like a professor. Can I just ask one more question?"

"One more."

"Why did you practically live at the library?"

"I was in love with my librarian's feet."

"Now that's a story I would love to hear."

"Fine, but let's get out of here. I've had enough of this place."

✤

"Nur, what did you whisper in her ear?"

"Must you know?"

"I'm so, so curious."

"I told her that he looks like a very good catch and that I wouldn't argue too much with him if I was her!"

"What made you say that?"

"Raqeem, didn't you notice how defensive she was getting? I wanted to distract her away from the tension that was building up inside her."

"She actually blushed."

"Only because I touched upon something in her that is genuinely attracted to Yune, and I don't just mean intellectually."

✣

They spent whatever was left of the night and much of the morning asleep at the Astoria. They slept in different beds and had very different dreams. Yune dreamt of Maryam holding Amanda's hand and walking away with her. And Amanda dreamt she was prostrating her head, as she once saw Muslims do on TV and as her head touched the floor, this beautiful feeling overtook her. She felt as though the very act of prostrating her head on the floor was somehow raising her entire body upwards. When she woke up, she shared her dream with Yune and immediately after made her shocking announcement.

"I want to become a Muslim."

"Amanda, please, don't speak like that. What we talked about last night was just another discussion like so many we've had before and so many we will have later. I'm not even a practicing Muslim. I never really was."

"Who's talking about you? You don't understand. I can't describe to you this feeling I experienced and I simply can't ignore it."

"But it was just a dream."

"No, it wasn't. It was more than I've ever experienced when I am awake!"

"OK. Why don't we just check out, get some breakfast and then maybe we can find a bookstore that has an English translation of the Qur'an. I think you should just take it easy and see how you feel in a week."

"Let's have breakfast. But Yune, you should know by now that when I speak with this certainty, I'm simply not going to change my mind."

Yune and Amanda went back to New Rochelle with an English translation of the Qur'an by Arberry. They were supposed to stay one more night in New Rochelle and then take a plane the next day to St. Paul from LaGuardia. That night, as Amanda sat in her room upstairs and read her new book, Yune did something he had not done in a very long time. He phoned Maryam.

"Hello Maryam."

"Yune? Is everything OK? Where are you?"

"Everything is fine. I'm sorry I'm phoning this late."

"Don't say that. What have you been so taken by?"

"Amanda!"

"Who's Amanda?"

"Amanda is the girl upstairs who has decided to become a Muslim!"

"What?"

Yune shared Amanda's story in full as he had observed it. When he was finished, there was silence. Finally, Maryam said:

"It may be just a passing whim. But if she's sincere, she will become something very difficult to handle."

"What do you mean?"

"I've met many converts here in LA, Yune. They carry a seriousness that is very hard for most people to deal with, especially someone as sensitive as you."

"Can I give her your number?"

"Of course, you can."

❖

The Gospel of Damascus

As they sat in the plane heading back to St. Paul, Amanda shared some of the verses of the Qur'an that touched her. She was fascinated by the story of Adam and Eve which, unlike its Biblical parallel, spoke of their repentance and, hence, did not advance a concept of original sin. Yune liked that subject. But when she started to ask him about what exactly one had to do to become a Muslim, he looked straight at her and said:

"Amanda, I'm not a practicing Muslim. It's true I have faith, and I'm very much at peace with how God is viewed in Islam, but that's all. I can't help you beyond that. In fact, I think you can be a Christian and a Muslim at the same time. I'm kind of like that."

"Well, I'm not. Why can't you just answer my question?"

Yune shook his head, reached into his pocket and took out a crumpled piece of paper which had Maryam's phone number scribbled on it. "Ask her," he said, as he turned his head to the window.

❖

Omar Imady

5

It was on the seventh of January, 1985 when a reluctant Yune and an emphatic Amanda got into a friend's car and drove from Grand Avenue to Columbia Heights. After an hour of driving through a snow storm and stopping at countless shops to make sure of the address, they arrived at a house that had been converted into a small mosque with a cafeteria in the basement. When they walked in, Amanda asked where she could recite her *shahada*, or the testimony of faith. A middle-aged man with a gentle face led them into the prayer hall. Amanda still had her head covered with her jacket's hood, so she wasn't asked to cover her hair. They sat on the carpet and as Yune watched the snowstorm through a glass window near the ceiling, Amanda repeated after the man:

"I witness that there is but One God, and I witness that Muhammad is his servant and messenger."

A tear fell out of Amanda's eye. Yune just stared at the window.

❖

After that event, Yune withdrew from his relationship with Amanda. He was too overwhelmed by the idea of her conversion. Amanda didn't pursue him; she had so much going on in her own world. By the beginning of the spring semester, she had moved out of her dorm and moved into an apartment with a few Malaysian girls who had eagerly adopted her. She stopped drinking alcohol all together, and pork wasn't a problem since she was a vegetarian. She also began to pray five times a day on a regular basis. The most striking change, however, was wearing a headscarf and dressing modestly.

It was early in February, when Yune saw Amanda for the first time with her new style of dress. He was talking to a few friends when he suddenly noticed that the three Malaysian girls who usually walked together wearing their colorful scarves were now four. But not really, that fourth girl wasn't Malaysian, that fourth girl was Amanda! The sight of Amanda wearing a headscarf seriously shook Yune's balance and brought back many memories of Maryam and her spiritual revolution ten years earlier. It was that linkage that I once tried to draw Nur's attention to that had the strongest impact on Yune. In a sense, what Maryam had introduced him to, was now once again being shared with him through Amanda. He had failed to cherish the legacy of Maryam, but was now being given another chance as it were. It's almost like the boat he had once missed had again approached his shore to see whether or not he was finally ready to embark. So much was at stake. Far too much to be drowned out by an Elvis Costello song and a weekend party with Chris.

By June, Yune felt as though his world, or his capacity to enjoy it, had been robbed from him. Everything out there, all that beauty that could be experienced at a liberal arts college like Macalester suddenly seemed tainted. His eyes, the way he perceived things, were taken over by Amanda. How long can a heart hold onto a stand which is contrary to one's perception?

Yune answered this question in July when he left his bed on a Sunday afternoon, walked out of his room and headed to the bathroom. For the first time in years, Yune made *wudu*, or the ritual of washing for prayer. The water was cold, and

Yune felt refreshed. He stood in his room and for a while tried to figure out where the direction of Mecca was. He had heard it was northeast. In a few seconds, he decided he should face the window. He locked the door, just in case Chris suddenly showed up. The thought of praying against the background of Costello's music was too much to bear. When his head touched the wooden floor, he silently prayed:

"My God, I'm so tired. I know I haven't been as close to You as I should have. But You know my heart has never betrayed You. I'm not sure I can really change. Help me."

Yune's "special prayer," as he would later refer to it, not only made him want to change in the way Amanda had changed but also made him want to bond with her again. But Yune's subsequent enthusiastic visits to Amanda were met with a formal response that he wasn't prepared for. He had expected Amanda to embrace him after hearing of his spiritual experience. Instead, as she stood outside the door of her apartment, she only smiled and said she was happy for him. Yune initially blamed her distance on the presence of the Malaysian girls, but eventually realized that Amanda had genuinely become far more formal when dealing with other men, him included. Yet, rather than abandon his own spiritual revolution, Yune proceeded to pursue it on his own.

He asked a few Malaysian friends who had rented a house near campus if he could stay with them and by September 85, he had said goodbye to Chris and 201 West Dupre. Yune also started to pray the five daily prayers on a regular basis, though he rarely could get himself up at dawn for the early Morning Prayer. Ramadan began in late May, and against his own expectations, Yune fasted the whole month. At times he would meet Amanda at *iftar*, or the special Ramadan dinners which were held at the basement of the chapel. They would smile at each other, but the thought of approaching her as she stood surrounded by all those Malaysian girls was out of the question.

By the spring of 1986, Yune had passed all the tests of sincerity he had confronted. And they were many. The most difficult involved women. A Mexican girl he once knew walking barefoot on Macalester's grass, calling out his name and asking him to join her as someone's radio blasted Prince singing "Purple Rain." Another girl at the Hungry Mind bookstore, asking him if he had ever made love to a woman who recited poetry during the act. And yet another girl at Kagin, the dining hall, who decided to pinch him as he stood in line waiting for his lunch! And, when asleep, dreams upon dreams of women he knew and women he had never met.

It was late in September, 1986 when Zahriman, one of the Malaysian students he was sharing the house with, handed him an envelope. "Yune, the American Muslim sister stopped by and left this for you." He waited until he was alone in his room to open it. It was a letter from Amanda. He read it carefully and after he had finished, he placed his head between his hands. Amanda had actually proposed to him. She wanted to marry him and begin a "Muslim family."

There are times when the most important decisions people make in their lives require no more than a few seconds of thought. This was such a time. Yune reached to the phone and dialed her number.

"Did you read it?"

"Yes."

"And your answer is?"

"Yes, my answer is yes."

❖

A wedding was planned for December. They would actually be two events, a reception in the basement of the chapel and a wedding ceremony in Amanda's apartment. Yune managed to convince his parents, Jane more so than Jawdat, that his marriage would actually motivate him to study even harder. Amanda's parents were still recovering from the dramatic change in their daughter's outer appearance when she broke the news. It wasn't so much her conversion to Islam that troubled them. Like Maryam's family before them, Amanda's parents couldn't come to terms with the headscarf. And now, this idea of getting married before graduating from college further increased their suspicion that their daughter, bright and special as she may be, was involved in something weird, perhaps even cultic. Ironically, the only comforting aspect to the whole idea was Yune. Amanda's mom had actually met Yune before Amanda's conversion and concluded, after putting him through the Midwestern ritual of a Trivial Pursuit game, that he was the antithesis of the stereotypical Arab male!

Maryam and Sarmad flew in from LA. Was it a coincidence that Amanda and Yune's marriage was scheduled to take place on their tenth anniversary? Sarmad was asked by Yune to perform the religious ceremony which in Islam did not require a clergyman, and the marriage was to be made legal at a later date. Ten years ago, Yune cried as he watched his first love being dedicated to another man. But on this night, Sarmad dedicated Yune to Amanda and Amanda to Yune. And no one was crying. But what exactly was going through Yune's mind on that cold winter night?

Angels do not have the gift of reading the thoughts of people. This is an accurate statement, but it needs to be highly qualified. The truth is we cannot hear people speak to themselves. But our intense intuition, dramatically stronger than the strongest possible level of human intuition, is rarely inaccurate when used to determine what is going on inside the deeper chambers of human minds.

Weddings can be experienced as events of longing, anticipation, joy, and passion. I have also seen them experienced as events of fear, doubt and even sadness. But Yune didn't fit neatly in any of the above, nor even in some type of peculiar combination. Yune, rather, was experiencing the event as though it was meant to save him. What was it he wanted to be saved from? From the sudden return of a Yune who would extract once and for all the tree that Maryam had once planted.

So strong was Yune's sense of the aesthetic that he could get into a bad mood for hours at the mere exposure to the sight of objects that lacked order, beauty or both. Yet, he wasn't offended by the ugly curtain which was put up to separate the men from the women in the name of an understanding of modesty which he never quite came to terms with. Nor was he disturbed by the sight of the shoes that were scattered near the door because religious Muslims, especially if they happen to be Malaysian, don't allow shoes to be worn inside the house. Perhaps most bizarre of all, was the American Muslim woman, married to a Saudi Arabian, who seemingly was the designated photographer of the event. Yet, she wore a veil over her face that revealed only her eyes and asked Yune and Amanda to pose for a picture session in the kitchen!

The mere hint that any of the people around him were uncomfortable would have, on any other night, sent Yune rushing to do anything in his capacity to alleviate their discomfort. But on this night, there were many who were very blunt about their discomfort, including Amanda's grandmother who could be heard complaining about having to sit on the carpet; Amanda's father, albeit more diplomatically, emphasizing the fact that Sarmad was not authorized legally to perform a wedding; and, of course, Amanda's mother who was so clearly baffled by what was taking place that she decided to remain silent but leave early.

Yune observed all of this, yet felt no impulse to make a move. If Yune was asked only a few months earlier to describe what his wedding would be like, he would have spoken of a Japanese garden with stone lanterns, lotus and koi ponds and small wooden bridges. Yune would have described an event where guests were treated like royalty and children walked around carrying white roses. Instead, Yune's wedding was taking place in a basement and children were either fighting or asking their mothers to accompany them to the bathroom. Only Amanda's rose dress, which unbeknownst to Yune was purchased by Amanda from a vintage shop on Snelling for a mere $62, was something Yune could identify with, but only because it had an untraditional color.

Yet tonight, none of this seemed to matter. The fire horse had left harbor, and nothing taking place on the boat was of any significance. All that mattered to Yune was where he believed the boat was heading – far and away from a life that didn't value God.

❖❖❖

Omar Imady

IV. A Box for Each Impulse

Omar Imady

1

Many are the paths he will explore.
But all will be blocked by a sealed door.
Sur– 10 years

Risha was in my cave when I broke the fourth cylinder. Never had I seen her look so sad.

"Sur? The day has actually come when I would rather it was Nur who would become the guardian of my child."

"You still think of him as a child?"

"In many ways, yes, I still do. But now I'm going to start thinking of him as a prisoner. A prisoner in Sur's kingdom!"

"Don't be so harsh on Sur."

"It's not about being harsh. It's just that it's so hard to visualize a horse, a fire horse, encountering a fence at the very moment it's convinced it's about to experience freedom."

❖

Sur wore glasses, silver glasses with black lines above the lenses, securing the effect of double eyebrows. He had a small head and very short, grey hair. Sur was looking through a microscope when I walked into his cave.

"I see you've become interested in bacteria?"

"What makes you assume it's bacteria? Why not green chloroplasts inside plant cells? Can you guess what shape they are?"

"No idea."

"Think of a shape I love."

"I didn't know you had a favorite shape."

"They're round."

"Are they?"

"Yes. You should have known I love to draw circles around things. Circling objects is my occupation."

"Well, it appears your talents are needed."

Perhaps it was Risha's words or my own sentiments, but it was quite difficult to provide Sur with the information he needed to take over Yune's life. I knew exactly where he was going to start. I could almost see his eyes contemplating a plan as I mentioned that Yune had just gotten married. Sur's first task was to demonstrate to Yune that there were definite limits to the experience of love among humans. In so doing, as Sur was well aware, Yune would quickly reach these limits, test the extent he could go beyond them and, once certain it wasn't possible, give up on the experience altogether.

Identifying limits for Yune's relationship with Amanda took Sur around a week. Yes, a week. All Sur had to achieve was to alter perception. To Amanda, the convert, Yune had to be seen as conspiring against her commitment to her faith. When he asked her to go out and have a romantic dinner with him, Sur made sure Amanda focused entirely on the fact that the restaurant served alcohol and, hence, it was not acceptable to enter such a place. When Yune purchased a dress, Sur made sure she became possessed by its failure to meet Islam's standards of modesty. To Yune, the poet and the believer in Bisher the Barefooted, Amanda had to be seen as not only unwilling to have an uninhibited relationship with him but also as insensitive, if not harsh, in how she articulated her unwillingness.

Watching Yune and Amanda argue wasn't pleasant, and I tried hard to avoid it. But my sense of responsibility toward the fire horse of the scrolls brought me back again and again to my screen. In response to his alienation, Yune sought refuge in a couch. Yes, a large green couch where he would spend most of the night flipping through channels as though it was some type of cathartic exercise. How ironic we must have seemed as I sat glued to my screen and Yune to his. At times, he would reach for a notebook and start writing a poem. Very few, however, were completed:

> *She came*
> *With a box for each impulse,*
> *A function for each desire,*
> *An antidote for each fantasy*
> *Mutating in a poet's mind.*
>
> *Until five o'clock*
> *I was searching for a home.*
> *Searching for a home in me.*
> *Now, finally, I am tired: Poetry and tea.*
> *I run to my shelter*
> *But it cannot remember me.*
> *On the floor falls perfection,*
> *A collection of war and insanity.*
> *A path dividing a cosmic sea:*
> *Poetry and tea.*

The arrival of Yune's first daughter, Fatima, distracted Yune emotionally, but had no real impact on how Amanda related to Yune or vice versa. Nor did graduating from Macalester and the family's subsequent move to Philadelphia where Yune had enrolled in a doctoral program in the department of Asian and Middle Eastern Studies at the University of Pennsylvania change the basic dynamics of the relationship.

Once content that he had set impenetrable limits for Yune's relationship with Amanda, Sur moved on to attack

Yune's newly-found religious experience. Sur clearly had a problem with anything that might hold the slightest sacredness in one's heart. Why? Because such a status is reserved only for God. Not even the very path that leads to God may be regarded too seriously; otherwise, one falls into a subtle form of associating an idol, intangible as it may be, with the glory of God. Once again, Sur knew exactly how to find his way into Yune's mind. Yune had a slightly obsessive compulsive tendency and was thus susceptible to what might be termed ritualistic mania!

Prior to performing their daily prayers, Muslims must make *wudu* or the ritual of washing for prayer. The whole process is supposed to take around three minutes. But Sur succeeded in transforming each *wudu* into a guessing game. Yune would constantly find himself asking if he had already washed his arms? His face? His head? Did he perhaps not make sure that water fully covered this or that part of his body, as is required? —only to go back and start the whole process again. At times, Yune would emerge from the bathroom after twenty minutes of struggling with water. All this ensured that his capacity to enjoy his prayers was hopelessly undermined. There was simply no room for a spiritual experience in the midst of all these concerns. When Yune finally stood to pray, not only were his clothes damp, he was often physically and mentally exhausted.

At the very moment Yune was experiencing his ritualistic mania, his tolerance for such behavior in others became increasingly depleted. I watched and wondered how Sur managed to replace the Yune that once associated the Muslim style of dress with strength and beauty with a Yune that felt it was nothing more than a dress code, a uniform! All Sur had to do was to strip it of the mental associations it once had with being embraced and unconditionally loved.

Yune would at times stand and observe Amanda carefully get dressed before leaving the house. The scene was full of irony, silent irony, but I could easily perceive it. Amanda felt each of the garments she put on, from the long pleated skirt and dark brown stockings to the sky blue coat she received as a gift from Maryam, served to reveal her true self. To Yune, on the other hand, the garments were concealing, not revealing, and their ultimate objective was to sacrifice his aesthetic sensibility on the altar of Amanda's modesty.

Amanda was also no longer interested in inquisitive talks. She had found what she wanted, and Yune's conversations often felt like word games she had no desire to play. Once as they were driving to visit his grandmother in New Rochelle, I watched Yune discover once again how resistant Amanda was to his thoughts and words.

"You do realize that all these rules you are following are just one specific strand in an ocean of different Muslim scholarly views?"

"What rules are we talking about now?"

"The way you dress, wash for prayer ..."

"I don't think your model of washing for prayer is something you want to talk about!"

"That's not the point."

"You do realize I'm driving?"

"Like why would you only wear a blue coat? How could that possibly be more modest than green?"

"Can we stop talking about my coat? When did I ever say it was more modest?"

"Fine, forget about the coat. Why is it so unacceptable to have a small Christmas tree in our house? Both of us grew up with Christmas trees."

"Christmas is all about celebrating the birth of the Son of God. Do you have any idea how uncomfortable that sounds to me? Did I tell you that even on my confirmation in my mother's Lutheran church, long before I ever heard about Islam, I couldn't get myself to repeat that part about the 'Son of God'?"

"Yes, you did tell me that story."

"You see, you know all my stories, why do you keep on challenging me?"

"But we don't have to see it that way; I never did see it that way. Why can't we just see it as the birth of the Christ?"

Amanda shook her head dismayed from Yune's persistence.

"Wouldn't you enjoy decorating a Christmas tree with Fatima?"

Amanda switched the radio on. It was Rush Limbaugh, the talk show host she so enjoyed hating. Yune turned his head to the back seat where Fatima was sitting. He looked at his three-year-old daughter and whispered, "You like Christmas trees just like your daddy?" Fatima smiled and nodded her head.

✧

2

After he graduated from Macalester in the spring of 88 with a degree in political science, Yune and his family moved to Philadelphia. Penn, a member of the Ivy League and the oldest university in America, carried an implicit promise of a highly-rewarding intellectual experience. Not only did Yune look forward to this experience, but he also, though not very consciously, regarded it as a compensation for his failure to experience the type of relationship he wanted with Amanda. But this was all before Dr. James Staks was assigned as Yune's academic advisor and, later, his dissertation supervisor. I often wondered if Sur had actually hired Dr. Staks. He was almost overly qualified for all that Sur attempted to achieve. Dr. Staks was a short man with broad shoulders and very thick eyebrows. His mother was Greek and his features were very similar to hers. So, too, was his temperament. Dr. Staks was infamous for his Mediterranean outbursts. Yune, on the other hand, was young and sincerely interested in knowledge. Nothing could have prepared him for the possibility that someone could tamper with his experience at Penn, let alone a university professor. Here, it wasn't Yune's potential for obsessive compulsive behavior that facilitated the trap. Rather it was his Arab politeness that made it very difficult for him to say no to people he was trained to respect. Syrian culture taught that teachers, in particular, demand overwhelming respect. As an Arab proverb proclaims: "Those who teach me, if only a mere letter, I will become their eternal servant." I'm not quite sure if it was Sur or Dr. Staks who noticed this trait in Yune first. But it was this trait that made everything that subsequently transpired possible.

Dr. Staks asked Yune to work with his team on a research project funded by the European Council on Turkish/Greek relations. But Yune had no clear terms of reference and quickly became the one who performed all the tasks no one else wanted to touch. Yune first felt honored for being selected, but four months later as he sat alone at Dr. Staks' office typing page after page of a meaningless study, he began to feel abused. The real fun started in mid-1990 when it was time to determine the exact subject for Yune's doctoral dissertation. It took literally six months for Dr. Staks to approve three sentences! The statement of the problem, or the *problematique* as Dr. Staks preferred, was rejected over and over again until Yune was close to giving up on the whole project. The most frustrating aspect of the whole exercise was the fact that what was approved in the end was almost exactly what Yune had proposed at the very beginning.

In the midst of Yune's emotional and intellectual frustrations, in the midst of that desert that Sur was constantly working on expanding, a small oasis was born that, to my surprise, was left alone by Sur. It was during one of those Muslim Student Association (MSA) dinners that Amanda loved to attend and at which Yune had to practice his version of self-hypnosis to survive, when Yune met a young man destined to become his friend to the very end.

Yune, though still years away from discovering an understanding of Islam that he was truly at peace with, was fully convinced by now that the vast majority of the Muslims he had come to know were not consistent with the most basic of his intellectual and spiritual ideals. The MSA dinners, for example, were hated by Yune because they were events where men, separated by a curtain from women, would meet to engage in diatribes against other Muslim sects, other religions and most importantly, the grand American Jewish conspiracy against them. Yune simply could not derive any additional self-respect or inner conviction from this type of activity. If anything, it made him feel like he was surrounded by hypocrites. Isn't America, he would wonder to himself, providing them with the freedom to hold Friday prayers on campus, to dress as they wish, to socialize as they wish, to pursue their intellectual objectives to the very end, and, yes, to have these silly dinners? Some have even settled in this country and purchased houses in American suburbs. They have barbecues in their backyard and carefully collect coupons. Yet, their faces beam with joy when they attack America. Yune wouldn't have minded, indeed, he would have fully agreed, if the criticism was of American foreign policy towards the Middle East. He regarded its approach to the Arab-Israeli conflict as overwhelmingly biased towards Israel, even when the most basic human values were at stake. But the words Yune drowned in during the early 1990s were categorically against America and all that it stood for. How he wanted to scream, "If you hate this place so much, why do you choose to live here?" But Yune, loyal to his sensibility, would remain silent and search instead for a quiet corner where he could spend the rest of the evening playing with the food on his plate. It was during one such evening while Yune was sitting alone in one such corner that a young man approached him and introduced himself as Tariq.

"You look like you're trying to escape. I don't blame you."

"I don't understand?"

"I think you do. You can't participate in their conversations. It's obvious. Don't worry; I can't either."

"Why not?" Yune replied as though trying to test him.

"When I do listen, I find myself unintentionally counting how many logical fallacies they are capable of coming up with. My lips start moving involuntarily: One; Two; Three. And then I panic and wonder if they noticed what I'm doing."

Yune broke out in laughter. Never before had he laughed at an MSA dinner!

"So what kind of fallacies do they create?"

"Where do I start? They compare the best aspects of their culture to the worst aspects of American culture. They are always searching for a conspiracy. They search for a conspiracy even when the available evidence is overwhelmingly clear that no such conspiracy exists. They are proud to base their objective conclusions on their subjective assumptions."

"Sounds familiar, very familiar. So what are you studying here?"

"Aesthetics."

"Are you serious?"

"Why wouldn't I be? What about you?"

"Well, it's just that I've met a lot of Muslims studying medicine, engineering and other scientific subjects, but aesthetics is definitely a first. I'm studying Middle Eastern Studies."

"I studied architecture at MIT and now I want something more theoretical. Middle Eastern Studies sounds very interesting too. What's your focus?"

"The role of civil institutions in the Modern Middle East. Where are you from by the way?"

"Egypt. But my ancestors are Circassians from the Besleney tribe. I've visited Besleney, it's a beautiful place. It's near Elbrus, the highest mountain in Europe. Have you heard of the massacre of the Mamluks?"

"You mean the one Muhammad Ali orchestrated against the Mamluks when he invited them all to his citadel?"

"That's the one, 1811, I believe was the date. Only one survived, Amyn Bek. He was my great ancestor!"

"You're kidding!"

"It's true; there's even this story that explains why he survived."

"He was well armed?"

"No, that wouldn't have helped him. Just before he headed to Muhammad Ali's invitation, one of his servants broke an expensive Chinese bowl. Rather than punish him, Amyn was very kind to him."

"And so he was protected?"

"Yes, he forced his horse to jump from the walls of the citadel and survived."

"This entire conversation, by the way, has a very surreal feeling about it."

"Yes my friend. My wife is not going to believe that I actually had a meaningful conversation with someone tonight."

Yune smiled. No one had called him "my friend" in a very long time.

And so a friendship was born. And in the basement of the house that Yune had rented on Conshohoken Avenue at the outskirts of Philadelphia, Tariq and Yune spent hours upon hours discussing subjects that ranged from Paul Riccour's approach to the absolute to Carl Jung's commentary on the *Book of the Cave* in the Qur'an.

Sur could not have overlooked this relationship. His decision to ignore it was undoubtedly very calculated. If I had to guess, I would say he was just trying to protect Yune from totally losing it. Yune's relationship with Amanda carried the promise of total existential blending and, hence, Sur felt he had to attack it. With Tariq, the relationship carried only the possibility of mental comfort. Tariq could talk when Yune had to be distracted from his mind which was pulsating with noise, and he could listen when Yune had to be distracted from his heart which was longing for a bond.

Of the various stories associated with Yune and Tariq, there is one that I truly enjoyed observing. It's one of the few nice memories I have of this entire phase. It was the summer of ninety-two when both Yune and Tariq were in the midst of writing their dissertations. Amanda and Fatima were in Damascus visiting Yune's family, and Raydana, Tariq's wife, and her son were in Cairo visiting her family. Tariq was staying in Yune's house and their plan was to finish three chapters of their dissertations before their families returned. This was the plan at least before Tariq showed up one evening with around ten foreign movies.

"You won't believe this, Yune. I found this place in Chestnut Hill called TLA. It has a fantastic collection of foreign *avant garde* movies—Fellini, Kurosawa, they have everything my friend."

"Are you serious?"

"I'm very serious. Serious enough to prepare us a great meal: sardines, onions, Tabasco sauce and Coke! All you have to do is decide which movie we are going to watch first."

Tariq climbed up the stairs to the kitchen as Yune removed the videos from the bag and carefully looked through them. In a few moments, he had narrowed down his choice to Fellini's *City of Women* and *8 ½*. He opted for *City of Women*, but as soon as he inserted the tape into the VCR, it suddenly occurred to him that what Tariq had initiated was the beginning of the end for all the academic plans they had made for this summer. Movies would follow movies, and after each movie, there would be a long philosophical discussion on what exactly the movie meant and before you knew it, the summer would be over and Amanda and Raydana would be back!

On the other hand, any attempt to try to reason with Tariq would be hopeless. He was in a Fellini mood, and no one would be able to get him out if it. Yune knew he had to act fast. He could hear Tariq climbing down the steps. He reached for a scissors on the table and, without hesitating, inserted it in one of the ventilation slots of the VCR. He removed it from the first slot and inserted it in another slot, doing his best to inflict as much damage as possible without changing the outer appearance of the machine.

"The feast is ready! Have you chosen our movie?"

"*City of Women.*"

"I like it. I like it. Let the show begin my friend."

Yune pressed the playback button and sat on the couch near Tariq. To his utter surprise, it worked. "How can it possibly work?" I could almost hear Yune wondering to himself. But it was only minutes into the initial scene, just as the train carrying Snaporaz was entering the tunnel, when the VCR stopped. Tariq had just bitten through a sweet white onion when his eyes opened wide in disbelief. For the next hour or so, Tariq tried everything he could to make the VCR work, but nothing could possibly repair the hidden damage inflicted by Yune's scissors.

❖

Omar Imady

3

Yune miraculously survived Dr. James Staks and received his doctorate in December 1993. Tariq finished around a year later. But already, by January 1994, Yune and his family had moved back to Damascus. The decision to return to Damascus was made years ago by Amanda. She wanted to be near the Shamsi spiritual order Maryam had so beautifully described. She repeatedly spoke to her friends of her desire to raise her daughter around women like Maryam. But this was intentionally not shared with Yune until it was clear to her that he had passed the point of no return in the writing of his dissertation. Only then, did Amanda begin slowly to introduce the idea. Yune's initial reaction was one of confusion. He just didn't realize how strong Amanda's attachment to the Shamsi path had become. Yune was also distraught about the type of job he would be able to secure in Damascus. His dream was to teach Middle Eastern Studies at an American university. To return to Damascus meant abandoning this dream. But eventually, Yune realized that it was a lost battle. Returning to Damascus was simply one of those things on which Amanda was not willing to compromise.

As Yune gradually got used to the idea of returning to Damascus, he had this dream. A dream that constituted to me, and in turn to my seven companions, the first glimpse of the task which Yune was destined to carry out; an image that could perhaps explain why this young man was so spiritually important. Yune dreamt he was an important official in Damascus. He wasn't quite sure what exactly his position was, but he was in charge of organizing a very important event that was to take place on Christmas Eve at the Grand Mosque of Damascus. Guests included ambassadors, high ranking officials, Muslim religious scholars, and representatives of every Christian denomination in Damascus. Yune was rushing from one place to another, trying hard to ensure that everything that needed to take place was in order. Then the scene shifted to the actual event. Around a stage set up in the large courtyard of the Grand Mosque were children, boys and girls, dressed in white and carrying white roses. Yune was now on the stage, ready to deliver an introductory speech of some sorts. But at the very moment he was about to speak, he woke up. Yune awoke very confused. He phoned Tariq and asked him to join him in the basement for an important discussion.

"So, how exactly am I to understand this dream?"

"Let's begin from the end. If you were supposed to know what exactly this event is about, you would not have awakened right before you started your speech."

"What?"

"Listen to me, my friend. Your speech would have given it away. The first words you would have spoken would have clearly addressed what this event was all about. But you woke up. And so we already know you are not supposed to know."

"Then why did I have the dream in the first place?"

"Because you have been arguing with your wife for so long now about going back to Damascus and you are convinced it's purely an Amanda project."

"It is."

"Listen to me. I think the dream is telling you that something very important is waiting for you in Damascus. You're going to be responsible for something so important that it will involve officials and ambassadors and even religious figures."

"But why the Grand Mosque?"

"Maybe, my friend, the Grand Mosque is just a symbol for Damascus. If they wanted to choose a monument that stands for Damascus, what could be more fitting than the Grand Mosque? It's like the Statue of Liberty for New York. But the point is it's not Amanda's project anymore. This is what you need to understand."

From that day on, Yune, who had already stopped resisting Amanda's attempt to take him back to Damascus, also stopped resenting her for wanting to do this. The project of return suddenly became a joint one. On the nineteenth of December 1993, when Yune and his family got on a Royal Jordanian plane heading to Damascus via Amman, Yune wondered if the sense of purpose that had eluded him in America would somehow be found in Damascus, the oldest continuously inhabited city in the world. But no sooner had Yune arrived in Damascus than Sur began his almost frantic attempt to ensure that nothing that Yune was destined to encounter here would provide him with any meaningful experience or sense of purpose.

First, Sur focused on the actual city. Yune had been frequently flustered by all the stories he would hear in Philadelphia about carjacking and drug-related shootings. Stories of women being kidnapped along with their cars in the middle of the day were not uncommon in Philadelphia during the 1990s. An Arab student Yune knew well who drove a taxi in the evenings was shot in the head, even after he gave his assailant his watch and wallet. A female student was raped in her own apartment, located only a block from campus. All this made Yune become overly protective of Amanda and Fatima. He was always worried when they were outside of the house, regardless of the time of day. One very special feature of Damascus which Yune looked forward to was how safe it was. But less than a week after his arrival, Yune was bombarded with a peculiar story that rivaled in its horror any of the stories he had heard in Philadelphia. The focal point of the story was a shop that sold dresses in the Qasa market, east of Damascus. A woman who wanted to try on a dress was led to a side room where she would be given a sedative injection. Only women who appeared to be on their own were targeted. A surgeon subsequently removed various organs from her body which were promptly and secretly transported outside of the country. Bodies were later disposed of at a faraway junkyard. The story was undoubtedly pure fiction. But Yune heard it and allowed it to take over his mind. And so, the image of Damascus as a place, safe enough to quiet the alarms of someone like Yune who worries too much, was completely destroyed!

Next, Sur turned his attention to the material objects of the new setting. Yune's father had purchased a house for the young family, a nice apartment overlooking a green field towards the end of the Mazzeh suburb. Everything about the apartment was perfect, everything except for this overwhelming smell of sewage that suddenly spread all over the house. Yune would race around from room to room, seeking to identify the source of the smell. He was almost certain it was coming from the kitchen, but there was nothing in the kitchen that could possibly explain it. He used every possible air freshener that could be purchased until Amanda and Fatima begged him to stop. Two years later, when a plumber arrived to repair a dripping pipe underneath the sink, the source of the smell was finally discovered. It was a pipe which was connected to the building's main sewage tank. The pipe had a cap, but it wasn't fully tightened and so when wind went through the tank, air carried the smell to all the connecting pipes, and the smell was suddenly released into Yune's house.

✣

"How could he possibly do something like that?"

"You didn't actually see him loosen the cap, Risha?"

"You know it was him, Raqeem. And don't start talking about his mandate. I can't see how filling someone's house with the smell of sewage can possibly be justified."

Yune also received a light cream Mercedes 200 from his father. It was purchased in 1990 and had hardly been used by anyone since. It had less than 4000 km on its meter. Yune loved the car and found compensation from the smell of sewage in his house with the deep scent of its leather. But the car had something very peculiar about it. As Yune drove along the highway, the car's engine would suddenly stop. Yune would then do his best to steer it toward the side of the road, often narrowly avoiding a serious accident. The car was sent over and over again to its main repair company in Damascus. Eager to please Yune's important father, the head of the company made sure German engineers supervised the check up. They found nothing that could explain the sudden engine failures. Only when the car was sent to an old Damascene mechanic was the problem finally identified. The engine was stopping because its supply of gasoline was suddenly terminated. A very small particle of rust was finally identified as the culprit. When it floated, the gas flowed uninterrupted, but when it decided to push itself against the small inner nozzle, the supply of gasoline stopped, and Yune found himself suddenly trying to steer his car to safety.

"This is criminal. And if I were you, I would summon Wahi and put him in the full picture of what's going on."

"Summon? Risha, you know I don't summon Wahi."

"Well, you sure seemed like you were contemplating it when I was trying to educate Yune. Do you realize he could have killed him?"

"It was rust, not Sur, which was responsible for the car suddenly stopping."

"Yes, a very innocent particle of rust that decided to block the flow of gas at precisely the moment Yune was driving on the highway. You can't possibly believe this!"

But nothing Sur helped orchestrate was more alienating to Yune than the type of job he ended up with. Yune wanted to teach. If he couldn't find a position at the University of Damascus then he wouldn't mind teaching at an international high school. But Yune's father, Jawdat, had different plans. Jawdat had returned to Damascus in 1985 to serve once again as a Minister of Economy. He would have loved to stay in Kuwait but felt blessed because upon his return he was able to secure the release of his nephew who had been imprisoned for being part of the Muslim Brotherhood. Jawdat learned from a UN official who had recently visited his office that the United Nations Educational, Cultural and Scientific Organization (UNESCO) had just opened a sub-regional office in Damascus. They are looking for a young Syrian who was Western educated. In fact, a vacancy has just been announced for a National Officer, the highest position available for locally-recruited staff. Jawdat was captured by the idea of his son working for the United Nations and proceeded to pressure Yune and everyone else who could pressure Yune, Jane, Amanda, and even Maryam, though still in LA, to convince him to apply for this position. Yune argued that this was, in the final analysis, a bureaucratic job that entailed managing people, concerns that were promptly dismissed by all. And so he applied, thinking the wise men and women of the UN would easily recognize that someone who consistently tested INFP, or "Introverted iNtuitive Feeling Perceiving" on Jungian personality type tests, could not possibly be suited for a job of this type. But Yune, with his doctorate from Penn, his perfect English and prestigious family connections, was recruited immediately. And so Yune became UNESCO's National Officer in Damascus. Yune preferred to describe himself as a dignified secretary/accountant/proofreader. He made appointments for consultants visiting Damascus, prepared the quarterly budget for the Office, and made sure all reports prepared by UNESCO's Syrian experts were free of grammatical and spelling errors.

Not only did Yune have to undergo all this, but this time there was no Tariq, or any other friend for that matter, to distract him. And whatever role Amanda could have played in protecting his sanity, Sur saw to it that her energy was directed elsewhere. Yune had hoped that once Amanda was in Damascus she would change toward him. Perhaps much of her emotional inhibitions could be explained by the fact that the convert within her felt threatened by America's non-Muslim environment, Yune would reason to himself. Perhaps once she is in Damascus, a predominantly Muslim city, she would no longer feel the need to have her defense mechanisms on such a high state of alert. Perhaps she would relax, and their relationship would experience a rebirth. Once in Damascus however, Amanda's intense longing for bonding with her Shamsi mentors and sisters meant that she would spend most of the day attending lessons, worship sessions, and various religious celebrations. Her degree in education also meant that she would be constantly sought to help out in the children's schools run by the Shamsi sisters. None of this was intentional by Amanda. She was not a co-conspirator with Sur, not consciously at least.

In less than three months after his arrival in Damascus, Yune came to fully realize that any illusion he may have once had about life in Damascus and the possibility however remote of a meaningful experience had been completely misconceived. Sur succeeded in transforming a regular day in Yune's new life in Damascus into one which began with waking up in a house that emitted sudden sewage scents, driving to work in a car associated with sudden and inexplicable engine failures, eight hours of fiddling with papers and inter-acting with colleagues who seemed to like to fiddle with papers, and then, finally, driving back to an empty home. Sur's thorough plowing of Yune's heart was completed. But how long could Yune possibly endure this?

❖❖❖

V. The Gospel of Damascus

Omar Imady

1

It was Christmas Eve 1996, when the fifth cylinder was finally ready to be broken. Risha was there, eager to see her child emancipated from the sealed chambers of Sur, a sentiment I confess to have felt as well.

A disciple will be sent to John. And the disciple will be
baptized with words. And the disciple will learn how to
breathe into birds.
Mizan – 2 years.

"Who is John?"

"I don't know, Risha. Come to think of it, one of the forty is named Yahya, or John. In fact, when Father Butrus died around six years ago..."

"Wait, who is Father Butrus?"

"One of the forty."

"Yes, yes, of course. Keep on."

"So it was Yahya, Yahya Nouri who replaced Father Butrus as one of the forty. It's all coming back to me now. Nouri is actually related to Sarmad!"

"Sarmad, Maryam's husband?"

"Yahya Nouri is Sarmad's uncle."

"The plot thickens. Well, it shouldn't be hard to introduce Yune to a relative, his brother-in-law's uncle."

"Yes, but the problem is Sarmad is still in LA, right?"

"No idea. Go find out."

"OK, will you do me a favor and inform Mizan."

"Are you sure he won't mind?"

"Mizan is all about balance and wisdom. Even if he did mind, he would greet you with a smile."

A few days later, it all had become clear. Yahya Nouri is one of the Masters of the Mevlevi Sufi order. He is highly educated, with advanced degrees in history and in religious law, but he is a very reclusive man who gives lessons to only a select number of disciples. Equally interesting, Sarmad, Maryam and their children are set to leave LA permanently and return to Damascus this coming Thursday. On Friday evening, Jawdat is holding a party to celebrate their return. Yahya Nouri is invited. So, too, of course is Yune.

"So, how did you make sure Jawdat would invite Nouri?"

"No, you got it wrong. It turns out Nouri is always invited. Yune should have met him ages ago. But Nouri never visits anybody!"

"So, how do we know he will come to this event?"

"We don't! But my feeling is, this is Mizan's domain. Let's just step aside and watch."

On Friday evening, at Jawdat Bukhari's house, men gathered in the large guestroom and women in the more informal living room. Relatives of both Sarmad and Jawdat were present. Yune was trying to keep busy with serving the coffee and the sweets so he could avoid having a conversation with anyone, a conversation that was bound to include the question, "How is work doing?" Suddenly, the doorbell rang. Yune opened the door and for a moment wasn't sure how he should act or what he should say. Standing in front of him were two men, both with something very royal about them. They both had short white beards. One was dressed in a black suit, the other in a dark blue cloak and a white turban.

Everyone stood up when Nouri walked into the guestroom. Jawdat rushed to greet him and led him to the most prominent chair in the room. No one asked or even seemed to wonder who the other man was. Perhaps they all assumed it was Yahya's companion. He was silent all night and he almost appeared as a bodyguard! Nouri spoke very little during the event, but as he was leaving, I watched him approach Yune and shake his hand.

"Yunus, visit me. Tomorrow evening is a good time. Sarmad will let you know how to get to my house. You will come, won't you?"

"Yes, yes," answered an almost hypnotized Yune.

Later I asked Mizan how he managed to convince Nouri to come to the Bukharis and in what capacity did he come along with him?

"I told him who I was."

"What do you mean you told him who you were?"

"I mean just that. I went to visit him, and the moment I sat with him, he told me I was an angel."

"He what?"

"He had me figured out in no time."

"And what did you say?"

"Well, I realized that this was a man of God with very strong spiritual intuition and that it wouldn't be wise to try to disguise the truth. So I just told him that yes, I am an angel. And that I was sent to ask him to accept this invitation so that he could be introduced to a young man named Yune."

"You told him all this?"

"Yes, and I even told him that he was to be entrusted with educating Yune for a period of two years."

"I'm not quite sure how to react. Had anyone else done this, I would be very worried. But how can I possibly accuse you of not being wise?"

"You're right. That wouldn't be wise."

I smiled and walked back to my cave. Risha was waiting for me.

"You look pleased."

"I am."

"But very ..."

"Consumed. All I can think about is Sunday and what exactly Yahya Nouri is going to share with Yune."

"Stop worrying," she said, as she gestured to me to sit next to her. Then, and for the first time, she placed my head on her lap and gently caressed my hair.

"Stop worrying, it's all going to be beautiful. I promise."

It was six in the evening when Yune knocked at the door of Yahya Nouri's home. Nouri was married but didn't have children or servants. His wife opened the door. She was wearing white prayer clothes and had a very strong voice. She referred to her husband as "The Teacher."

"The Teacher will be with you in a minute," she said as she directed Yune to the guestroom. The guestroom was reminiscent of my favorite reading room back in Seattle. True, it's around a hundred times smaller. Yet, it had two beautiful arches, and the wall facing the south and separating the room from the balcony was made entirely of Damascene carved wood and colored glass.

Yune sat on a couch and stared at the floor as though wondering why he was invited here and why on earth he so willingly accepted the invitation?

"Because you're supposed to learn how to twirl," Nouri proclaimed as he entered the room.

"Twirl?"

"Yes, let's find out if your heart can dance." Nouri removed his black cloak, exposing a beautiful white flowing robe. With his left foot acting as a weight-balancing pillar, his right foot began moving in a slow circular motion. He raised his hands in the air and tilted his head to the right. Nouri was performing a slow version of the dance the Mevlevi order is so famous for. "Don't hesitate," Nouri said, and Yune didn't. He stood up, stared for a few seconds at Nouri's movements as though trying to figure out the essential steps, and then started to twirl, careful not to invade Nouri's space. Beams of light of various colors fell upon the two moving figures, and for the first time in years, I felt Yune smiling from within.

Lessons, December 1996 – December 1998

On Yune's first visit, Nouri gave no religious lectures like Yune had expected and feared. On his second visit, however, Yune brought with him a new notebook—large and green and reminiscent of notebooks Maryam once gave him—and truly hoped Nouri would talk about his spiritual path and Nouri did. His words totally unraveled the various complexes Yune had towards his religion. And so Yune's experience of prayer, including the ritual washing that preceded it, departed the realm of the obsessive compulsive to the realm of tranquil mysticism. His discomfort with legal ritualism was replaced by an attempt to experience its subtle logic and symbolism. This was the magic of Nouri's words. They aimed at deepening one's experience of faith, and they achieved this even when, as Yune would later discover, their reader was a Jew, Christian, Buddhist or Hindu.

Everything that Nouri wanted to convey, he did so through a form of poetic prose that was rich in metaphors and that often left Yune and me both captivated as well as not quite sure we had fully understood all of its implications. Yune would return home and rewrite his notes in a more organized way, often making connections that didn't come to him as he was listening. What Yune produced in the process was a fascinating spiritual manifesto, brief and concise, yet dramatic in its implications. He even gave it a title as though he already knew it was destined to be published. Yune was very careful not to include anything which he didn't believe Nouri would approve of. Unbeknownst to Yune, a time would come when many of Nouri's acquaintances would emphatically deny that Nouri could have possibly endorsed such views.

❖

Omar Imady

2

The Gospel of Damascus

A Manual of Faith for the Ends of Time

The Words of Yahya Nouri

(Compiled by Yunus Bukhari)

✣

An uncompromising monotheistic sensibility of the heart will rise in the third millennium as the spiritual bond of the global community of believers. It will uphold an invitation to every member of the human race to have a direct personal relationship with the God who created this entire universe from naught! An invitation that does not entail casting aside the discoveries of science or the principles of universal human rights.

A direct relationship with the Creator of the billions of galaxies and all that they contain. From the snowflake to the supernova. What is an individual human heart in front of such glory? Yet it is invited to have a direct relationship with God who is both completely transcendent and at once overwhelmingly immanent. How special we must be to receive such an invitation.

For thousands of years the vast majority of humans couldn't relate to God except through the mediums of sculptures, images and even people; righteous and otherwise. Later, they needed Hellenic mythology to help mediate the idea of pure monotheism. But this invitation implies that none of this is necessary—especially now. It implies that our hearts, insignificant as they may be, are equipped with the capacity to experience the majesty of God: "The heavens and the planets failed to embrace My Majesty and yet the heart of my believing servant succeeded where they have failed."

❖

Then escape now unto God from all that is false
(Qur'an 51:50)

Around 1418 years ago, our Prophet and his companions undertook a *hijrah*—a departure. They left their homes in Mecca and traveled to Madinah. Abraham began his spiritual journey with a departure. Moses and the children of Israel also undertook a departure. Egypt was where the seeds of their faith were planted. The Promised Land was where the tree bloomed. At times, such departures entail crossing physical distance, but they always entail crossing spiritual distance.

So ask yourself, where are you now? Has your heart departed yet? Are you still in Mecca? Have you arrived in Madinah? Or are you perhaps somewhere in between? You need a manual for your departure – a manual that will guide the child within you out of the cellars of your world.

First, you need to know what you must leave behind. It's really a very simple equation: everyone & everything that refuses to come with you. Next, you must determine what you will bring with you. Over time, departure-experts have realized that it's impossible to leave without a companion to hold your hand and a guide to hold your heart. There are a few things that many bring along—maps, a compass, and a watch—but eventually they discover that they are useless, if not distracting.

But most important, you must know why you have departed. People depart for different reasons. Some depart in hope of more wealth, power, or status. Some depart for a beautiful woman or an attractive man. Some have more subtle types of objectives. Perhaps they are drawn to the glorious image of an idea. Perhaps they want to be regarded as part of a glorious project. Or perhaps they are simply following someone who wants to be on this path. Everyone is allowed to depart. But after a day of traveling, a month, a year—at times even decades later, that very objective, that hidden intention, is suddenly transformed into a large wall blocking their path. Observe the irony! The only way to keep walking on this path is to cleanse yourself of the very objective of your journey. Some turn back. Some spend whatever is left of their lives trying to penetrate the wall. They cannot. This wall cannot be penetrated! Yet, it can disappear, but only if those types of objectives are cast aside. You see, only one type of objective or intention is permitted on this path: love. Love of what? It doesn't really matter. True, sincere love is of one source, and it always leads to the same place. Love anything you wish and be truly loyal to this love. This experience of love will then lead you to the love of God. The more loyal you are, the faster it will take you to the only One worthy of such intense and complete love. Have you experienced this type of love?

Before your heart falls in love, you must first have a heart. The Qur'an states: "This is a reminder for the one who *has* a heart." Everyone is born with the heart that pumps blood. Its activity is consistent, involuntary and indispensable. The heart that pumps love in a consistent, involuntary and indispensable way is not something you are born with; it's a gift that is born under very specific conditions.

My heart was born when I was around twelve. I was on my way back home when I noticed a few boys my age harassing a kitten. They were trying to chase her into a corner. I wasn't the type who could scare anyone. I didn't have the body or the personality for that. But when I approached them, I just screamed. I screamed until they all ran away. I still wonder why my voice had that effect on them. Then it was time to take care of the kitten. My first impulse was to carry her home, away from the dangers of the road. But then it occurred to me that she was so young. I had heard my mother mention once that a recently born kitten cannot survive without her mother. I was so confused. If I leave her, the boys may come back and harass her, and if I take her home, she may not survive because I deprived her of her mother. Finally, I decided to just sit there on the pavement and wait until her mother showed up. I waited four hours. I was hungry and tired. I was about to give up when I noticed the kitten rushing toward another cat. It was her mother, and my duty was over. At home, I was shouted at and sent to bed without dinner for having disappeared like that. But I had a very sweet feeling in my heart, and I slept smiling.

Years later, I shared this story with my teacher. He told me it takes around four hours for a heart to be born. Four hours of doing something caring and compassionate that makes absolutely no sense to anyone, not even to your own self.

❖

*And remember the Name of your Lord and
devote yourself to Him completely.*
(Qur'an 73:8)

The Gospel of Damascus

Once a heart is born, it has to learn how to breathe; otherwise it will suffocate under the darkness of your own neglect. The Qur'an states: "It is not the eyes that go blind; but rather it is the hearts ..." Only *zikr*, or spiritual meditation that has as its objective direct communion with God, will teach your heart how to breathe.

Do you remember how Moses was first selected? Moses was searching for fire to keep his family warm when instead he encountered the burning bush which immersed the earth with light. I wasn't searching for *zikr* when I first encountered it. It seems it was searching for me. My uncle had sent me to find a chimney cleaner. It was late fall, and the house was getting cold. But the chimney was so full of soot that it was unhealthy to try to light a fire. When I finally reached the shop of a famous Damascene chimney cleaner, way up on Mount Qasiun, I found his shop locked. A man standing nearby told me that I could find him at this mosque even further up the mountain. So, I headed towards the mosque. I didn't know what this man looked like and I was too embarrassed to ask anyone in the mosque because everyone seemed so consumed with their prayers. I sat in one of the corners of the mosque, exhausted and disappointed. Then I heard a man saying, "Come sit next to me." He was an older man with a white turban on his head. He gestured to me to take hold of his hand. Then he said, "Close your eyes, take a deep breath and observe your heart repeating, without moving your tongue:

> *God is with me*
> *Watching me*
> *Witnessing me*
> *God is with me*
> *Watching me*
> *Witnessing me"*

And I did. Then he asked, "Can you see the name of God engraved inside your heart with white light?"

I looked within, but all I could see was darkness. I felt as though I was standing on the roof and looking down our dark chimney. I wanted to open my eyes and let go of his hand. But he pressed my hand harder and asked me to take a deeper breath and to focus more this time. Suddenly, I saw something, vague and dim, but nevertheless, I saw something, something resembling a white flame that took on the shape of a word. Was it the name of the One God? Was it in Arabic script? Was it Allah? I was still trying to focus on this image when the old man said: "Don't be consumed by the word. Move from the name to that which the name refers; allow yourself to contemplate that majesty." He said this, and I felt as though I had an electric shock. He let go of my hand and with a comforting smile, he quietly said: "As you lie in your bed, observe your heart repeating the words I taught you until you fall asleep. Now, my son, you can move on to cleaning chimneys. The man you are searching for is standing near the window." It's been sixty years since that day, and as my teacher once instructed me, I haven't slept once except in a state of *zikr*.

❖

So he acquired poise and balance.
Being on the higher horizon.
Then he drew near and drew closer.
Until a space of two bows or even less.
Then He revealed to his servant what He revealed.
The heart distrusted not what it beheld.
(Qur'an, 53:6-11)

You cannot walk on this path unless your heart knows how to listen to the divine voice. To some, the Qur'an is a book of law. To others, it's a book of theology. And yet to others, it's a manual for the struggle between the forces of light and the forces of darkness. But to those who walk on our delicate path, the Qur'an is a record of those sacred moments when the divine voice spoke through a human heart.

First you have to appreciate what this means spiritually. Once I asked my teacher, why is it that the Qur'an may begin with referring to God in the passive pronoun 'He', then suddenly shift to 'We', 'I', or even 'Me;' and perhaps later return to 'He'? My teacher was silent for a few seconds as though to determine whether or not I was spiritually mature enough to hear the answer. Then he said:

"When your heart engages with the verses of the Qur'an, it becomes extra sensitive. And so 'He' is invoked as a distancing device. The 'We' brings you closer, but it is still royal and formal. Then the 'I' appears and shakes the ground underneath your feet; only for 'Me' to arrive and completely melt you: *If my servants ask you oh Prophet concerning Me, tell them I am indeed close …*

But the 'I' and 'Me' are too intense to be sustained by our fragile hearts and so, the verses return to the less direct 'We' and 'He.' If your heart is truly engaged with the voice of the Qur'an, the 'I' can make you tremble like that moment when you first tasted love but far sweeter."

There are many other ways to taste the spiritual implications of what it means for the divine voice to speak through a human heart. The Qur'an relates the story of Mary, the mother of Jesus. It's an intense and beautiful account. In the midst of the story, you suddenly encounter a verse that appears inexplicable: "And you weren't with them when they cast their lots to determine who amongst them would be entrusted with Mary." We know the Prophet wasn't with them. The Prophet himself knows he wasn't with them. Why then does this verse suddenly appear? The same verse appears in the midst of the account of Joseph and thrice in the account of Moses.

But the mystery is resolved once your heart begins to listen. This verse appears because the divine voice had lifted the Prophet to such a state of transparency that the Prophet now can clearly see the events being revealed to him. It is as though he is standing next to Zechariah, the father of John the Baptist, as he takes hold of Mary's hand and leads her to the Temple. It is as though he is walking along with Moses as he enters the city of Midian. It is as though he is standing next to the brothers of Joseph as they plotted against him. But the divine voice suddenly interrupts the narrative and proclaims: "And you weren't with them ..." It is almost like the Prophet is gently being brought back from where the eyes of his heart have carried him; and then, having protected him from ascending too high, the divine voice resumes the account.

None of this can be understood by simply reading the text. You must allow your heart to experience the words.

Once you are able to experience the Qur'anic voice, the true message and intended purpose behind the verses of the Qur'an will begin to unfold.

Your mother may shout at you at times. She may try to calm you down. She may be harsh and she may be gentle. She may make rules, and then she may choose not to enforce them. If an outsider was to hear her, he would most likely misunderstand her completely. But not you. You don't need anyone to teach you how to listen accurately to your mother. You don't because your heart is engaged with hers, and so you know the true purpose of her words. She may threaten you, but you know she really just wants you to behave yourself. What she guides you to do when you are a child, may change completely when you are a mature adult. If you are about to fall she may pull your arm so hard that it may hurt for days, but you know, you know deep inside that she was just trying to protect you. All of this we understand and experience with our mothers. But the God who created us loves us far more than our mothers are even capable of. Why is it that when it comes to God's words to us, we so easily remove them from the context of love?

The Qur'an is a record of how God spoke to us through our Prophet's heart not only in different circumstances, but also at different stages of our spiritual evolution. Yet, scholars come and tell us: "This is what the Qur'an is saying and these are the laws it upholds." But all of this, all of their books of theology and law, are based on *reading* the Qur'an with eyes and minds, rather than *listening* to it with our hearts. The Qur'an teaches us that it is inside the heart where true comprehension takes place: "Or do they have hearts through which they can comprehend things?" If our scholars were to truly listen, most of what they have recorded in their books would have to be dramatically revised. If our scholars were to truly listen, a spectacular reformation would begin. Close your eyes today and start listening with your heart.

❖

O my servants who have sinned in abundance. Do not despair of the mercy of God. Indeed, God forgives all sins. He is the Most Forgiving, the Most Merciful.
(Qur'an, 39:53)

Far more profound than all of these books of theology and law are two stories which our Prophet shared with us: They summarize our entire path. One is about a cat, the other about a dog! A woman who dressed modestly, prayed and fasted was not invited into the bliss of Paradise. Why? Because she failed to care properly for a cat that lived in her house until it died of hunger and thirst. The cat died and so, too, did the woman's spiritual worth in the eyes of God. Her

145

modesty, prayer and fasting were for naught! Another woman sold her body for material profit. She didn't commit such an act out of passion or love. No, she sold her body for a few silver coins. Once, as she was traveling, she found a well and decided she would fetch water for herself. She suddenly noticed a thirsty dog and, just as she fetched water for herself, she fetched water for the dog until its thirst was quenched. This woman was invited into the bliss of Paradise. She wasn't even seeking forgiveness. Yet, she was forgiven, and she became special in the eyes of God.

Sin humbles us. It humbles our hearts. But if we are stubborn and we go too far, it can also burn us. Most of what religious laws ask us to refrain from has now been explained by science. Everything that is proven medically to be harmful to our bodies should not be part of our lives. But those sins are less, far less, than the sins we commit against each other. The sin of mistreating a cat, let alone a human being, can forever block you away from the majesty of God.

❖

And from water, We made all that is alive.
(Qur'an, 21:30)

Once your heart is humbled by sin, it will become like water, always seeking to disappear into the lowest parts of the earth. There is so much we can learn from water! You must be as lenient as water. Observe how it takes on the various shapes of the objects it is poured into without changing its true nature in the process. Be as persistent as water. Observe how it falls upon a rock, century after century, until it reduces it to sand. Be as wise as water. Observe how it evaporates when the weather is hot and how it returns back to earth in the form of rain when the weather is cooler. Be as embracing as water. Observe how when it falls from the sky, it falls upon the shacks of the poor and the castles of the rich. Be as loving as water. Observe how its dew kisses the grass at dawn. Once you become like water, everything that touches you will come to life.

❖

Proclaim to them: Everyone is waiting in anticipation for the events they believe will unfold.
(Qur'an, 6:158)

Our Prophet spoke of the ends of time. He described minor signs and major signs. All the minor signs have been fulfilled. We are now at the beginning of the final stage. The final stage may last years, and it may last centuries. Only God knows how long it will last. But we are now at its beginning. Many are those who realize this. They are burning with anticipation. But what are they waiting for? Victory? Justice? A better world? You can tell a lot about a person if you know what exactly he is waiting for.

To live in the ends of time is to live in the age of Christ. It is to live in a state of waiting for his return. The return of the Christ is the most important of the major signs. It will eventually lead to the end of war and the culmination of our human civilization. An age when we will become everything we are supposed to become. Our Prophet says, "If anyone amongst you is still alive when Christ Jesus the son of Mary returns, say to him: Our Prophet sends you his greetings of peace."

But the earth needs to be prepared for this event. So much needs to be done. Significant changes must take place in the way people think and feel. Most of these changes will be taken care of. The forces that will lead to these changes have long been at work. And yet, very important tasks remain untouched.

Just as it was in the age of the Christ, our world today is being taken over by a Roman empire, a new Roman empire. An empire that respects humans, their freedoms and their intrinsic rights, yes. But also an empire that does not respect the sacred, that is spiritually depleted, that has lost its sense of purpose. And just as it was in the time of Christ, this empire is home to four major groups, each with their own object of waiting.

First, there are those who are preparing for a final battle. They are waiting for a military victory against this new Roman Empire. They come from different religions but they are united in this purpose, in this hatred. Yet, the age of Christ is about life, not death. A victory will take place, but it will not be a military one. The son of Adam once said to his brother, "If you are to raise your hand to strike me, I will not raise my hand in return and strike you. I fear God, the Lord of the Worlds." We are finally ready to grasp these words, to cast violence aside. It took the development of nuclear weapons for us to finally realize that the age of violence must end or we will end with it.

The second group is the law protectors of this age who are waiting for a time when the religious laws they have devoted their lives to articulating are adopted by a state that applies them in their entirety. They are waiting for a legal victory. But most of the laws they have articulated have lost touch with their intended purpose. And while these scholars are still disputing legal matters which have nothing to do with the lives we are living today, we are losing entire generations of believers to materialism.

Those who have been lost are the third group. They are the most numerous of all the groups. Millions upon millions of people have been lost to materialism. They wait; indeed they strive, for the day when they can become full citizens of the new Roman Empire.

The Gospel of Damascus

And then we have the fourth group, the group that embraces those who are waiting for the righteous teacher who will guide this world out of its darkness—who are waiting for the Christ. True, the new Roman Empire will be victorious over all its enemies. But it will be taken over from within by the new followers of Christ, just as his previous followers permeated the first empire with light. Among this group are the select few who will play a special role when Christ returns, who will be there to welcome him in Damascus. This is a task that remains untouched!

✢

Jesus, the son of Mary, will descend on the White Tower,
east of Damascus.
He will be carried by two angels, his hands holding on to
their wings.
When he raises his head,
droplets of water will fall like scattered pearls.
(Prophetic Tradition)

✢

There will be among the followers of our Prophet successors to the Disciples of the Christ. But these disciples need to be identified, their hearts need to be captured, and their lives must become an experience of intense anticipation. If I were young, I would go out and search for them. And when the Christ descends on the White Tower, east of Damascus, when he arrives in layers of light, I would hope I was there to kiss his hand and whisper, "Oh Prince of this age, the seal of all prophets sends you his peace."

Omar Imady

God was pleased with those companions who made a covenant with you under the tree ...
(Qur'an, 48:18)

A covenant of faith unites members of this fourth group. It is a covenant that not only cuts and polishes the diamond, but it's also the sealed box that will carry it through the Ends of Time:

> *We will uphold and respect the oneness and majestic transcendence of God and we will open our hearts to experience God's presence and love.*
>
> *We will devote ourselves to selfless giving that we may be blessed with real hearts.*
>
> *We will depart the paths of materialism and we will do so for love.*
>
> *We will instruct our hearts to breathe before we fall asleep.*
>
> *We will listen with our hearts to the words of our sacred books.*
>
> *We will be humbled, though not burned, by sin.*
>
> *We will embody the secret qualities of water and seek to give life to everyone who crosses our paths.*
>
> *And we will master the art of patient and tranquil waiting for the arrival of the Prince of this age, the Christ.*

✣

3

Early in December 1998, Nouri died. After the funeral, Yune returned home and sat on his favorite couch which faced a large window overlooking Darayya, a town west of Damascus. He didn't speak and stayed more or less fixed to his couch for three full days. Amanda wondered if she should consult a doctor. But then he took a long shower, got dressed and headed to his office.

It was Nouri's lesson on waiting for Christ that convinced Yune that he had a role to play in preparing the earth for the Second Coming. My companions on Mount Hermon and I agreed and felt that we finally understood why this person we have been consumed with for the last thirty-two years was so important. He had a role to play in that task that "remained untouched," the task of identifying successors to the Disciples of Christ who would be there to welcome him when he returned. Suddenly Yune and we, the Guardians of the Design, were on the same page.

❖❖❖

Omar Imady

VI. Prepare the Way of the Lord

Omar Imady

1

*Eleven will be found drifting in the shade. Twelve will be
there when Damascus is remade.
Asa, Rahma & Risha – 12 months.*

"Sounds like a numerical code!"

"Whatever it sounds like, the sixth cylinder has brought
me back."

"Yes. But why Rahma and Asa?"

"Asa to give Yune authority, Rahma to give him the power
of captivating hearts, and I to give him the power of tickling."

"A fascinating combination. To be used for what purpose?"

"That's for my intelligent Raqeem to figure out. As long
as I have access to my Yune again, I'm over the moon."

"The moon?"

"Yes, the moon, it's a human expression," Risha said as
she pointed to the sky and moved her head up and down like
a child would to confirm an idea.

"Put the moon aside for a minute Risha and help me with
these numbers. First eleven, then twelve?"

"Listen, it must have something to do with what Nouri
said about identifying the Disciples of Christ."

"So Yune will set out and identify eleven, using authority,
love and seduction to facilitate his task. He identifies eleven
and, once he joins them, they become ..."

"Twelve! But where will he find them?"

"Where he spends more than eight hours every day."

"UNESCO?"

"Where else Risha? He hardly knows anyone in this city. He's either at home or at work!"

"Fine, so your job is to come up with possible entry points for Asa and Rahma into UNESCO."

"And you?"

"Don't worry about me. I'll have a job there by tomorrow."

By March 1999, all three had secured important UNESCO connections. Both Asa and Rahma in the form of special consultants. Asa was to prepare a report on secondary education, and Rahma a report on female empowerment in contemporary Syria. Both had to visit the office often to provide progress reports and use the small library on the upper floor. The actual report that Asa and Rahma were entrusted in preparing was a spiritual genealogy and an emotional biography of every man and woman, whether employees or consultants, who worked with Yune at UNESCO or even just visited the place. It's not that I didn't trust Yune in selecting the right disciples, but my mandate was to ensure the right choices were being made and the information provided by Asa and Rahma would help me confirm this. Risha, on the other hand, was now the new receptionist. No one entered the office or left, no one placed a phone call or received one without having to go through Risha. During the nine months that followed, from March to December 1999, Yune, as witnessed by all my Mount Hermon companions, applied himself fully to his task. His performance, albeit enhanced by the presence of Asa, Rahma and Risha, was always passionate and often breathtaking.

❖

The Gospel of Damascus

If Yune were to be asked to identify the most important feature of the disciples he was seeking, he would have answered, "They have to be children!" Several poems he wrote elaborated on this metaphor.

You know you have become a child
When your heart is full
And your hands are empty.

Children live in the forgotten corners of this world.
In the ruins of temples, churches and mosques, you will find them.
Tested, subdued, their eyelids fused.
Hiding in the shadow of the sun.
Underneath the northern ice, you will find them.
Celebrating their nothingness.
Eager to confess their weaknesses.
And blending their paths into one.

It was a room.
Like those found in hospitals.
Not far from the corridors
leading to the sirens of intensive care.
It was a room.
Like those found in pyramids.
Sealed from light, yet desecrated by all.
Adorned with the hymns of an ancient faith.
Buried underneath the sand dunes of noon.
It was a room.
And it was a child's heart.

In his attempt to identify these children, Yune was to quickly realize that they were not to be prepared by him. Indeed, they were to be discovered. Every single one of them had already been selected and, over time, sculpted, polished and refined. The primary difference between them and Yune was the fact that they were unconscious disciples; unconscious not only of who they were but also of what they were meant to carry out. Yune's task was to discover what was already there—what was not, no charm of his could seduce it into existence. Yune came to understand this not as a theoretical concept that he sat and reflected on, it came to him rather through a painful personal experience.

For during this very time period, Maya, the Maya of his teenage years in Kuwait, suddenly and unexpectedly reentered his life. This came about through a sudden phone call which interrupted an otherwise uneventful March afternoon. She just wanted to say hello, she said. She had met his mother the day before and got hold of his office phone number. She now lived in Beirut and worked for some type of graphic design company. She may have wanted to just say hello, but Yune perceived her phone call as a dramatic sign. She was going to be the first successor to the Disciples of Christ. Four weeks later, after many crossings of the Syrian Lebanese border, after many evenings in Beirut's artists' hideouts, not to mention phone conversations lasting hours and hours, after all this, Yune fully tasted those words once revealed to the Prophet of Islam in the midst of his eagerness to convert his uncle to monotheism: "You do not guide the one you love, indeed it is God who guides whomsoever He wills."

Ironically, Maya resisted Yune's invitation, but she did not resist Yune; making it even more difficult for Yune to comprehend what exactly was taking place. In a matter of days, Maya seemed willing to let go of her entire life to be with Yune, the very Yune who had abandoned her fourteen years earlier. She spoke of a departure to Norway, a new beginning for both of them, a therapeutic time in the Norwegian wilderness but the moment he started talking about Christ and the Second Coming, she would smile and look away, "Did you really come back into my life to talk to me about Jesus?"

An additional complication was the fact that Maya had all those beautiful traits one naturally would associate with spirituality; depth, kindness, and a poetic sensibility. "How do you bring a spiritual person to spirituality?" Yune would often ask himself as he drove back on the Beirut-Damascus highway. But Maya's spirituality was not open to anything remotely associated with religion. And no matter how many windows Yune succeeded in opening inside of her, he still could not convince her to look out of these windows and observe the sky.

Four weeks later, Yune finally understood that crossing to the other side requires more than the availability of a bridge and a guide. The disciples he was seeking have been waiting their entire life for the moment when they were invited to cross. They may not be aware of this intellectually, but all you have to do is share the idea and recognition would take place. Maya heard the idea repeatedly and dismissed it repeatedly. Beautiful and pure as she was, she was not one of the twelve. Four weeks later, Yune's attention shifted elsewhere.

✛

Even after all this time in Damascus, Yune had no real friends. He did, however, have many acquaintances, most of whom were colleagues at the UNESCO office. So it was natural, or perhaps meant to be, that he would focus his attention on identifying disciples among his colleagues. Knowing Yune's discomfort with pretentious men in positions of authority, it was not surprising to see him focus on his female colleagues and on those men who held very humble positions in the office. But in the end the disciples broke down evenly, six women and six men. Not counting Yune and the eleventh disciple, whose religious affiliations were as mysterious as his identity, five were Muslims, and five were Christians, including Catholics, Protestants and Orthodox. By national ancestry the following countries were represented: Syria, Palestine, Egypt, Spain, Germany, and Russia. But Yune of course had within his very lineage African, Asian, European and American ancestors.

❖

Yune's classification of the ranks and titles of the disciples:

Tariq al Kashef
The Twin of Yune's Heart

Prophet Muhammad once described Abu Bakr as the only one among his companions who accepted his message without any hesitation. No temptation of any sort, no promises were needed; no inner obstacles had to be overcome. Such was the case with Tariq, the man Yune befriended at the University of Pennsylvania. Tariq now lived in nearby Amman. Early in April, Yune asked him to visit Damascus. When they met, Yune, without any type of introduction, asked him: "Will you wait with me for the Christ?" Tariq immediately answered: "What else would I possibly do?"

The Three Daughters

Also in April, Yune made a covenant with three female disciples. In his eyes, they were 'daughters,' daughters of very special men. Sofiya and Raydana were daughters of the Prophet Muhammad via the lines of al-Hasan and al-Husain; and Eva was the daughter of a very special religious reformer, Banudi Sanqin.

Sofiya al-Hasani was a descendant of the Prophet through the line of his elder grandson al-Hasan. On the day she joined the disciples, Yune felt as though he had been given a price-less diamond. Sofiya headed the HR section at UNESCO. When not working, she always was reading a book. One day as she was reading Kafka, Yune sat with her and spoke to her about Christ. She remained silent. The next day, Yune found a folded paper on his desk. These were the words it contained: "No one could have entered this place because this door was not there earlier. It was created only for you. And now I'm going to close it."

❖

Raydana al-Husaini was a descendant of the Prophet's younger grandson al-Husain. She was also the wife of Tariq al Kashef. Tariq spoke to her constantly about waiting for the Christ until she agreed to meet Yune. After arriving in Damascus, she asked to sit with Yune alone. She had always felt she could tell if anyone was speaking the truth. It was a quality she believed she had inherited from her grandfather, the Prophet of Islam. Tariq left them in Yune's office. After an hour he returned, anxious and hoping his wife had let go of her resistance. When he entered the office, Raydana was holding Yune's hand. "I'm with you—all of me is," she said to Tariq and reached out to him with her left hand as her right hand held tightly to Yune's.

❖

Eva Sanqin was the great-granddaughter of Banudi San-qin from rural Homs. Late in the 19th century, Banudi met a Presbyterian evangelist in Damascus and converted to Pres-byterianism. Upon his return to his village, his Syriac Chris-tian community accused him of heresy, but he stood firm and succeeded in converting his two brothers. "This new path," he would say, "is more in touch with waiting for my Prince, the Christ." A century later his great-granddaughter stopped by UNESCO to borrow a book from its library. There she met someone who spoke to her of a path that was more in touch with waiting for Christ. As Yune took hold of her hand, she whispered: "I know it's hard to believe, but in sixty minutes you have entered the very place in my heart where my children reside. I will be loyal to what you have shared with me till the very end."

The Two Flames

In May of 1999, Yune found two more disciples who quickly became inseparable from him. Anytime he turned around, at least one of them was always there. Yune regarded them as flames he could always count on no matter how dark or stormy it became.

Nabeel Sidiqui

Nabeel Sidiqui was a middle-aged man who ran errands and made coffee and tea for UNESCO employees. Everything in his life was ordinary; his background, education, and house. His wife was the only non-ordinary component of his life and only because of how systematic her abuse was of her husband. Nabeel hated confrontation and found refuge from being insulted at home in a small mosque in Rukn al-Din where an *imam* named Shaikh Ahmad spoke to him about being an ambassador for true Islam in an age when most Muslims were distorting their faith. True Islam, according to Shaikh Ahmad, is above all 'prestigious.' It's prestigious because no matter what religion you belong to, you can't help but be impressed when you observe it in action. "Nabeel, if they are not impressed, if they don't think it's prestigious, then there's something wrong with how you are representing it—or even worse, there something wrong with how you understand it." And so there was nothing more distasteful to Shaikh Ahmad than those Muslims who committed acts that not only made others see Islam as not 'prestigious,' but as ignorant, violent and barbaric. This was how Nabeel loved to spend his evenings, listening to Shaikh Ahmad speak of a prestigious Islam that is worthy of guiding human civilization into an enlightened spirituality.

Nabeel, as is the case with all the disciples, had to undergo three stages of selection: Initial, preparatory and final. We angels are well aware of this process. Final selection is not to be confused with either initial or preparatory selection. The path begins with initial selection, moves on to preparation and then a question is asked and on the basis of how the question is answered, final selection is confirmed or withheld.

The initial selection of Nabeel Sidiqui was based on the fact that he represented the only living male descendent of St. James, the brother of the Lord. Neither Nabeel nor any of his recent ancestors were aware of this grand connection. In the tenth century, Ilyas, a great-grandfather of Nabeel, left his family home in Jericho after his brother married the young woman he secretly was in love with. Ilyas settled in Damascus where he would eventually convert to Islam and marry the daughter of his neighbor, a deeply religious man who looked after Ilyas as though he was his very son. From his children he concealed all of his past connections, all except for his special love for the Christ and a determination to live a righteous life. St. James was known as "the Just," and a millennium later, Ilyas would become known among his fellow Damascenes, as Ilyas Sidiqui, or Ilyas the Just.

Nabeel's preparatory selection was completed on that night when he walked back to his home feeling as though he had received a royal decree from Shaikh Ahmad designating him as an elite spiritual knight mandated to share pure monotheism with the world. He arrived home and did his best to open the door without waking up his wife.

"You know what I'm going to do tomorrow? I'm going to that mosque of yours and I'm going to expose you right in front of your sheikh! I'm going to tell him how difficult it is for you to provide for this family, maybe then he will realize that he is wasting his time on you."

His daughter in the nearby room began to cry. Nabeel wondered if she had heard his wife scream at him. Every cell of his body wanted to scream back, wanted to tell his wife that he had had enough. But his anger was interrupted by a question, a question he heard in the very voice of Shaikh Ahmad, "Would it be prestigious to scream back at her?" Nabeel paused for a few seconds, and then rushed to his daughter's bedroom avoiding any eye contact with his wife. His daughter glanced at him and then closed her eyes. He placed his hand on her head and sang in a very low voice:

"Allahu Allah Allahu rabi, awni wa hasbi, mali siwahu, mali siwahu–God is my lord, my helper, my sustainer. I have no one to turn to except Him, I have no one to turn to except Him."

To Yune he would once confess, " … when I sing, only my mother knows I'm crying … "

✢

From the very beginning of Yune's employment at UNESCO, Nabeel felt drawn to Yune. No one smiled at him like Yune did. No one asked him why he seemed tired, sad or even happy other than Yune. And no one asked him to sit and drink the very cup of tea he was serving other than Yune. With Yune, Nabeel would become the higher ambassador he felt he was. And with Yune, he would share the words Shaikh Ahmad shared with him. And Yune would smile and tell him how much he agreed with these words. And so when Yune shared with him his vision of the coming Christ, when the question constituting Nabeel's final selection arrived, Nabeel felt as though he had been promoted from an ambassador of true Islam to a successor to the Disciples of Christ. The promotion was prestigious and Nabeel embraced it in full. And hence, his final selection was confirmed. From that day on, Nabeel loved to be around Yune, hoping that he could be helpful in any way at all. He remained mostly quiet and in the background, but if Yune needed anything, he would jump to the task.

Nabeel played an important role in convincing Rakan Madi, Yune's personal assistant, to be one of the disciples. But Rakan, as later events would confirm, joined more out of his desire to not be left out of what appeared in his eyes as Yune's circle of influence. Much of the trust Yune placed in him was eventually betrayed.

Alisar Cozak

Alisar was the niece of Nadeen, a Christian woman who worked in the research unit at the UNESCO office. Yune felt close to Nadeen and was seriously contemplating inviting her to join the disciples when she surprised him with a request. She said she wanted him to meet her nineteen year-old niece who was severely depressed. "She wakes up screaming every night! There's something about you Yune that calms me down, perhaps you can help Alisar too?"

Alisar was medium height, with black hair and an hourglass-shaped body. And her style of dress drew attention to her strong feminine features. When she walked into Yune's office early in May 1999, she was wearing a long skirt with a slit on each side and a tight T-shirt that was short enough to reveal her navel.

"So why did you ask to see me?" she asked as she sat down on the small couch facing Yune's desk. She was full of confidence and completely at ease looking straight into Yune's eyes.

Yune smiled. "It was beyond my control."

"Are you interested in me?"

"Yes. And in ways that may surprise you."

"I've never slept with an older man. In fact so far I've only slept with a pillow."

"A pillow?"

"Yes, we have a serious physical relationship. It even has a name. Juan. You know, from Don Juan."

"So you place your head on Juan and then what?"

"No, there's another pillow for my head. Juan sleeps between my legs. And then suddenly, in the middle of the night after he makes sure that I'm fast asleep, he makes love to me."

Yune turned his head to the window on his right. He wasn't uncomfortable and that surprised him.

"You know what's even more intimate than making love to someone?"

"Surprise me!"

"Sleeping in someone's arms."

"I don't have trouble sleeping."

"You don't. But then you suddenly wake up with your heart racing. You know you've just had a nightmare, even though you can't remember anything. Then you drown it all in Juan."

"Nadeen told you this?"

"Nadeen doesn't know this. I can get rid of the nightmares."

❖

Alisar stood up. She walked towards the door and closed it. Then she approached Yune until she was standing right in front of him. Yune remained calmly seated on his chair as though he already knew this was going to take place. Alisar bent down, placed her hand over his eyes as though to block his perception of what she was about to do. And then she kissed him. It was a long kiss. Her tongue pushed its way into his mouth and before she moved her head away, she gently bit his lip. Then she uncovered his eyes as though to examine her effect on him. Yune's eyes were still closed. Alisar could tell, as well as I could, that Yune had somehow deflected the impact of her kiss.

He whispered: "I can get rid of the nightmares."

"Make love to me and I'll get rid of Juan."

Yune smiled. "What are you doing this afternoon?"

"Nothing if you want to see me."

"I do. Let's meet at five."

"Yes, where?"

"Let's meet here and then we can take off."

Alisar returned at five. Yune was waiting outside in his car. He saw her arrive in a taxi and called out to her when she approached the main gate of the UNESCO office. She turned around and headed to his car. She was now wearing a sleeveless dress, white with small red roses sprinkled on it. Her high heeled slippers drew more attention to a manner of walking that appeared naturally sensual.

She climbed in and her hand immediately reached to Yune's leg. "Are we about to betray Juan?"

Yune remained silent and drove towards the old city.

"You've heard of Bob Dylan?"

"I should be asking you that. You're too young to know Bob Dylan!"

"Well I happen to be a fan. If you want to turn me on, put on some Dylan."

Yune looked to his left and examined the spot in the door's pocket where he placed his CDs.

"I'm afraid turning you on is going to have to wait."

"Don't worry; I can imagine it's on."

"You can? What are you listening to?"

"Mr. Tambourine Man."

To the north of the Citadel, there's a small alley that had recently been renovated. Yune drove through the arch and then stopped the car. He closed his eyes and recited the Fatihah, the opening chapter of the Qur'an.

"What are you doing?"

"Abu al-Darda', the first Muslim Judge of Damascus is buried here. I was just sending him a prayer."

"Do you own a house around here?"

Yune kept driving. He took a right then left and then parked the car.

"Come."

Alisar followed him. The Grand Mosque was a few steps away. Yune headed to the tourist gate. He purchased a tourist entry ticket and asked for a *jilbab*, a hooded gown which women who were not dressed modestly were required to wear inside the mosque. He handed it to Alisar.

"Are we going to make love in the mosque? I don't mind if you don't?"

Yune reached for her hand and walked in the direction of Bab al-Faradis located below the northern Minaret of the Bride. He took his shoes off and placed them with the guard of the gate and gestured to Alisar to do the same. He paused to take a look at her. The black hooded gown and the bare feet gave her a very different look, but failed to erase away her natural sensuality.

This time Alisar reached to Yune's hand as though this had become a natural move between them. The courtyard was fairly empty. A few children running around and chasing the pigeons. A few women sitting in the shade and talking. Yune walked right towards the Dome of the Treasury. He sat with his back against one of the columns.

Still standing, Alisar said, "Here? This is not going to be very comfortable!"

"Just sit Alisar. Now look up. The minaret to your right will very soon witness the beginning of something so remarkable that it will change the very nature of human civilization."

"All I want to do is kiss you again."

A few pigeons approached them. Then they seemed to hesitate. They cooed at each other. Then they came closer. Others followed. Soon Yune and Alisar were surrounded by pigeons.

"What do they want?" Alisar said loudly.

"They want you to behave yourself." Yune answered with a smile.

"Tell them to go away."

This time Yune placed his hand over her eyes.

"We need to put Juan aside for a moment."

Alisar felt a spring breeze brush against her face, the cold marble floor underneath her bare feet. A wave of sleep suddenly arrived. She tried to resist it. Yune's hand and the sweet distant sound of children laughing didn't help. She stopped resisting. Her head fell on Yune's lap. Her body curled up. She shoved her hands in between her knees. A courageous pigeon approached her feet and then hopped on her leg. Yune smiled, wondering how Alisar would feel if she was suddenly to open her eyes. Asleep she remained until the sunset call for prayer broke the silence. Alisar opened her eyes.

"You must have drugged me."

"It was the pigeons. Any dreams?"

"Yes, but no nightmares. That's it I'm replacing Juan with you."

"Juan will not be pleased."

"I'll get him a female pillow."

She drew close to his face, Yune was afraid she was going to kiss him again right there in the courtyard of the mosque. Her mouth was now right next to his ear. "Cast your dancing spell my way, I promise to go under it."

✣

Alisar Cozak was born in Damascus. But her ancestors once roamed the vast steppes of Ukraine. The Cossacks were passionate freedom lovers and Alisar had clearly inherited these traits. After the Russian civil war ended in 1920, many Cossacks, who had earlier sided with the Whites, left Russia. Most headed toward other European countries, and even America and Canada. But Andri, Alisar's great-grandfather chose to head toward Turkey and subsequently Syria, settling in the northern town of Kafroun. His decision was based on a dream in which a voice asked him to head to Syria and find the Mountain of the Virgin Mary. He found the mountain near the northern town of Kafroun. He purchased a small parcel of land, built a home and got married to the daughter of the village baker. One day as he worked on his farm, he found himself wondering what if? What if he had left for Germany like most of his relatives. Wouldn't life there have been easier? How could he have made such an important decision on the basis of a mere dream? These questions got louder and louder. He slept early that night, hoping to escape the noise. That night, he dreamt he was shown a young girl, a beautiful young girl. She was wearing a diamond crown, even more brilliant than those worn by the Tsaritsa. He asked "Who is she?" And the answer came: "She is your descendant and she is why you were brought here." Andri woke up with a beautiful feeling. He didn't understand what exactly the dream was referring to. But there was something so special about it that was sufficient to stop those regrets once and for all.

✣

That afternoon in the courtyard of the Grand Mosque marked the beginning of a new Alisar. Like her great-grandfather before her, she didn't quite understand what exactly Yune meant with all his talk about the coming Christ, but there was something about him deep enough, strong enough to dispel her dark side. That vulgar sensuality that fed on a dark relationship with her imaginary friend Juan, gave away to repentance and a light sensuality that expressed itself in a gentle almost innocent manner.

Even more so than Nabeel, Alisar followed Yune everywhere. Once during a trip to Aleppo for a UNESCO related mission, he returned to his hotel room late at night only to find her sitting in the corridor next to the door of his room.

"You are late!"

"And you are in the wrong place."

She followed him in.

"I'm very sleepy; I can't believe you kept me waiting this long."

"Alees," as Yune would refer to her "I didn't even know you were in Aleppo!"

"And you call yourself intuitive!"

Yune headed to the bathroom and when he came out, she was already lying in bed. He shook his head and climbed into the bed next to her. She placed her head on his right arm as a young daughter would with her father.

"Please hug me. I can't wait to dream in your presence."

There was a time when I would have immediately pulled Yune, Alisar or both of them out of that bed. But I wasn't worried. Everything in that room was innocent; everything seemed to be in perfect balance.

The Traitor

In addition, there was Yune's personal assistant, Rakan Madi. The disciples would later refer to him as the traitor. Yune would avoid speaking of him, but when pressed, he would say: "He was the one who was invited to dine in the King's chamber and chose instead to eat in the stable."

The Three Pillars

Alejandra Menendez

Alejandra was a Spanish woman in her early twenties who was stationed in Damascus as a JPO or a Junior Program Officer. She was one of a very small number of young men and women who were selected by the Spanish government to be trained in the UN system and eventually absorbed by various UN agencies as international civil servants. Like the rest of the disciples, Alejandra was also one of only twelve, selected from all living humans to be there when the Christ arrives.

Proud as Alejandra was of her Spanish heritage, she was not aware of just how interesting that heritage was. One of her maternal ancestors by the name of Elgira was amongst a group of Spanish women kidnapped by the troops of Uthman Ibn Naissa, the Berber governor of northern Iberia in the eighth century. Hours later, the frightened sixteen-year-old Elgira found herself in the tent of an Arab soldier, Jawwad Ben Umair. When Jawwad saw her face, he paused, clearly not expecting this type of beauty. He then reached into a box and took out an emerald ring. "In the name of the One," he said as he placed the ring in her trembling hand. She had never seen a stone so green. As Jawwad made love to her on that cool spring night, her hand held tightly to the ring and her lips constantly repeated a prayer. Jawwad placed his ear against her mouth, as though trying to inhale her words along with her scent. Only one week later, Elgira was freed and by the end of that very month of May, she was married to Sancho, one of the young Asturian men who were responsible for her escape. In nine months, a daughter was born. Elgira named her Gibelurdin, a mushroom with a bright green underside. This female child, born to a bond solemnized in the name of the One and consummated to the prayer of "Christ is my Redeemer" was the great maternal ancestor of Alejandra Menendez.

Four centuries later, on the 16th of July 1212, Diego López, a direct descendant of Gibelurdin, fought in the Battle of Las Navas de Tolosa, known in Arabic as al-'Iqab or the Punishment, a major Spanish victory and one of the milestones of the *Reconquista*. Later, as Diego walked between the nearly one hundred thousand bodies of the killed and wounded, he heard a faint plea for water. To his right, a Muslim soldier lay on the ground clearly in his dying moments. The sun was setting; Diego was exhausted, slightly wounded himself and eager to leave the battle ground. But something in him took over his fatigue, his desire to rest, his eagerness to celebrate this victory; something so strong that it made him rush all the way back to the main camp to fetch water and return. As he carried the small jug of water, he was frightened he would arrive and find the Moor had already died. "Who are we, what do we stand for," he asked himself as he ran back "if we fail to respond to a dying man's wish for some water?" When Diego arrived, he raised the man's head and placed the jug of water near his lips. But the man had already died. His last contact with water was destined to be the tears that fell from Diego's eyes on his cheeks. It was in the name of that moment that Alejandra, a twentieth-century descendent of Diego, was honored with becoming a successor to the Disciples of Christ.

Alejandra was around 5'2" and had the body of a young teenager. Her hair was dark chestnut and her eyes, an interesting shade of pine green. Her very short skirts, though always very stylish, made her seem like a school girl walking around the office. She was eager to have someone in the office involve her in a meaningful project. But she had a strong Spanish accent and she spoke so fast that most Syrians in the UNESCO Office, who knew English only as a second language, had difficulty understanding her. Yune was aware of this communication problem and used it to his advantage. So, when he phoned her to ask if she would come by his office, he could already sense how much she longed for attention, professional or otherwise.

"Have a seat. What would you like to drink?"

"It's not like I have a lot of options, Yune!"

"We have excellent cappuccino!"

"Cappuccino? I haven't had Cappuccino since I arrived in Damascus."

"Well, it's time to do something about that. Follow me, Alejandra."

Yune said this and walked out of his office without even bothering to look back to make sure Alejandra was following him. But she was. And in moments they were in his black Sangyung Musso which he had purchased around a year ago after deciding that his Mercedes was fit only for a museum of technological abnormalities! And as Bruce Springsteen sang, "You can't start a fire, worrying about your little world falling apart," Yune steered his car far and away from the UNESCO Office. Moments later, they were at the Sheraton, one of only three five-star hotels in this city. The lobby was architecturally inspired by grand Damascene-courtyards and it even had several fountains. In one of the corners, a young woman played the piano. Yune walked towards a somewhat secluded corner and gestured to Alejandra to sit. A waiter arrived out of nowhere and two cappuccinos were ordered.

Yune observed Alejandra. She had a sleeveless white shirt, a maroon skirt and white shoes with high heels and red butterflies which she wore over her bare feet. To his left, a few meters away, a woman sat alone reading. She was wearing a red sleeveless shirt, a white short skirt, and high-heeled red shoes with white butterflies. Her image entered Yune's eyes, and then, seemingly unable to fully comprehend it, he returned to Alejandra with an enhanced, even excited level of attention.

"I've never been here. You're completely crazy. Why did you bring us here?"

"I thought you wanted to have cappuccino?"

"Yune, we are supposed to be at work, aren't we?"

Alejandra had a way of keeping her lips slightly open after having just finished asking a question. There was also a hint of a smile. This would last for a second or two then her tongue would appear, touch her upper lip and would disappear again. Yune noticed this and so did Risha and separately they both thought that there was something sensual about this. This was important because up to this point, Yune was not sensually inspired and he was at his best when not only motivated by a sense of purpose but also emotionally engaged and sensually inspired.

"Alejandra, how can we work together if we hardly know each other? Tell me something about you."

The cappuccino arrived. Alejandra was in a hurry to taste it as though to comfort herself that she was indeed here for a purpose.

"This is good. I'm surprised. What do you want to know?"

Again a few seconds of lips parting, the appearance of the tongue, and the final effect of wet lips.

"Everything."

"Okay. I'm from Spain. You already know that. But what you don't know is that I'm from Asturias, the most special part of Spain, the only part that was not conquered by the moors!"

"Interesting."

"We are a proud people and we make the best *sidra* in the world."

"*Sidra*?"

"*Sidra* is cider. We have the best apples, and so we have the best cider!"

"I'm still waiting to hear about you. Shall I help?"

"How will you help?"

"By asking you specific questions."

"Ask."

"Have you ever been in love?"

"Yune! These are private matters."

"I'm just trying to know you better. If you want, we can finish our cappuccino and leave."

The thought of leaving was very unpleasant to Alejandra. Yune may be asking about "private matters," but she was engaging in her first real conversation since she had arrived in Damascus, and she was willing to talk about anything to prolong it. And so, two hours later, Yune and Alejandra walked out of the Sheraton. Yune was still a mystery to her, but she had shared with him stories and secrets her own sister didn't know. But there were stories that she chose not to share; stories that had to do with her relationship with her stepmother. Alejandra did not share with Yune her stepmother's physical abuse which continued all the way until she left for Damascus. She did not share that evening when her stepmother slapped her face in the presence of her friends because she didn't like the way she was dressed for her nineteenth birthday party. Nor did she share the day when her stepmother beat her with a hair brush for daring to ask her to speak a bit gentler to her father. And most importantly Alejandra did not share the way in which she constantly responded to this abuse, "I'm sorry I upset you, I promise I won't do it again." Perhaps Alejandra didn't share these stories with Yune or anyone else because somewhere in her unconscious she understood them as secrets that could be shared only with God. Collectively, these stories constituted her preparation phase and when she finally arrived in the lobby of the Sheraton, she arrived carrying a deep sense of that feeling found amongst those who respond to their wounds with grace. It is a feeling of certainty that they will one day be healed.

Later that evening, Yune phoned her. She was at her small apartment in Abu Rummana.

"Are you ready?"

"Ready for what?"

"Have you forgotten our date tonight?"

"What date?"

"Fine Alejandra, if you don't want to go ..."

"Wait, I want to go. Where are we going?"

In twenty minutes, he was at her apartment, a studio on the roof of a building in Abu Rummana. She opened the door and rushed back to her bedroom to finish getting dressed. Yune caught a glimpse of her bare feet and white shorts. He walked in and headed towards the terrace.

"You can change the music if you wish."

It was Rosana and the song was "Descubriéndote." Repeatedly listening to this song was soon to become Alejandra's favorite way to spend her evenings as she reminisced at her times with Yune.

"Do you know what she is saying? Or is your Spanish as bad as my Arabic!"

Yune turned around. Alejandra wore a short black dress, black thong slippers, and lots of silver objects including a toe ring.

"She is saying, 'I've been looking for you for a long time, in my soul and in my skin.'"

They ended up at The Piano Bar, located on the road leading to the Chapel of Annanias where Paul, nearly two thousand years ago, was cured of his blindness. Alejandra was in a playful mood, there was something about Yune that had attracted her, yet she was not sure what it was exactly. But Yune, the child once educated by Risha, responded to her playfulness with sophisticated elusive seduction which served only to further enflame her. When she asked if he would like to go back to her apartment, he spoke of having an office party there. When she asked what his favorite fantasy was, he shared with her Plato's allegory of the cave, and when she placed her foot on his, he reached down and removed her toe ring. "Where did you get this from, can I try it on?"

On their way out, she seemed like she had run out of energy. She placed her arm around his waist and tilted her head towards his shoulder. Yune walked her in the direction of the chapel. The Chapel of Annanias closes at around six, but the gate was still open when Yune and Alejandra arrived near midnight. I wondered who was responsible for this. Was it Asa? But Yune seemed to take it for granted. They climbed down the dark stairs until they reached the underground chapel, once the basement of Annanias' home. A few candles were lit, emitting enough light for some of the icons on the wall to be visible. Alejandra crossed herself, then stood in awe and repeated:

"Cristo es mi redentor;" Spanish for 'Christ is my Redeemer.'

She then turned her head towards Yune.

"In one day, you have opened me up like I never have before. And now you bring me here. My soul has now opened up to you just as much as my body had earlier at the bar."

Yune remained silent.

"What do you want from me?"

"I want you to wait with me."

"Wait? Wait for what?"

He whispered against her ear:

"Wait with me for the Christ, the son of Mary, the eternal virgin, who is sent by the One God of all. Be with me when he descends in glory on the White Tower, east of Damascus."

Alejandra stared at Yune in complete shock. Her hand reached to his shoulder as though to stop herself from falling. She wasn't sure if he was actually expecting her to respond. She then gathered all her energy and walked back quickly towards the car without saying a word.

They didn't speak as Yune drove her back home. Alejandra seemed totally dazed. When they arrived, she climbed out of the car and walked toward her apartment building without saying goodbye. Suddenly, she turned around and headed back to the car. Yune opened the window.

"Do you remember what I told you about Asturias?" "That it was never conquered?"

"Yes. But tonight Yune, less than an hour ago, the Moors have finally entered Asturias."

Yune smiled. "Perhaps Alejandra, but they did so in the name of Christ!"

Hans Siebold

Dr. Hans Siebold specialized in cultural literacy. He knew so much about the history of Damascene culture that he often left Yune intellectually enchanted. Once as they were walking through a vegetable market in Rukn al-Din, Hans asked:

"Dr. Yune, do you realize why the figs are called *Baali* figs?"

"Because they're rain-fed."

"Yes, but why *Baali*?"

"I don't know, I just assumed it's the word for crops that are rain-fed."

"Baal is the god of rain, thunder and lightning. We actually know the story of how he became the god of rain from tablets found in Ras Shamrah in northern Syria which date from about 1500 B.C.! So, you see, the point is that more than 3500 years later, after centuries of Judaism, Christianity and Islam, figs that are rain-fed are still referred to in Damascus as the figs of Baal! What does that say about Damascus?"

Hans was born in the Rhineland, in the village of Urmitz. His father, Johannes, was a Stabsoberfeldwebel, or a navy technical sergeant, in the German army. He had a background in engineering and so he was sent to supervise the construction of German fortifications in the Norwegian port of Bergen. On a short vacation in 1940, Johannes married and his first son, Hans, was born nine months later. Once the fortifications were completed, Johannes was asked to supervise the construction of another project, the Espeland concentration camp in Arna, not too far from Bergen. Workers, many of whom were Jews, were brought in from the Ulven concentration camp. It was then that Johannes started to have these dreams. The theme was recurrent, he was always involved in building something, some type of building which at first seemed glorious but towards the end of the dream would always catch fire and burn to the ground. One morning, still recovering from yet another variant of this dream, Johannes witnessed a soldier beat one of the workers to death. Suddenly and unexpectedly, the two images converged, the fire of the dream with the violent beating of the worker and out of this something was born in Johannes; something that made him possessed with redeeming himself for having helped build this 'house of evil,' as he came to see it. From around 1943, to 1945, when the Espeland camp was liberated, Hans not only had helped over ten Jews escape to

Sweden, but most importantly, had consistently shared his food rations with prisoners of the camp. "How many loaves of bread," he would ask himself, "does it take to atone for building this place?" Many of the two hundred prisoners who were found alive by the camp liberators, owed their survival to Johannes Siebold. But Johannes disappeared before anyone could thank him. He took off his uniform and found his way back to his family in Urmitz.

As a child, Hans remembers when his mother took him to visit the Cathedral of Cologne. He was told that what looked like a golden cage contained the preserved relics of three Persian kings. These three kings once traveled in pursuit of a star that took them all the way to Bethlehem where they met the Christ child. Years later, he traveled to Cologne with his neighbor Helga to attend the opening of the Opera House. It was a grand event and Wolfgang Fortner's *Die Bluthochzeit* or *The Blood Wedding* was spectacular. Yet Hans remembers clearly how he left Helga during the intermission and walked across the street to the Cathedral. It was closed, but all Hans wanted was to stand in silence near the Cathedral's gate and close his eyes.

Before turning to sociology, Hans wanted to become a priest. Perhaps it was his mother; perhaps it was those afternoons he spent at St. Georges' church repeating the rosary. But whatever it was, it wasn't enough to carry him through the experience. And so instead of continuing his theology studies at Trier, he gathered his savings and decided to explore North Africa. Once, as he walked through a market in Marrakech, he noticed a small mosque. He had visited the grand mosques of Marrakech, but this was different. The *asr* or afternoon prayer was already over and the mosque was closed. Hans instinctively found a back door, and walked inside. It was shaped like a small square topped by a dome. Circling the base of the dome was stained blue glass. "This is really different," Hans whispered to himself. He sat with his back towards the wall and in moments was in deep sleep. Half an hour later he woke up and left the place. The Hans that eventually would meet and believe in Yune was born during those thirty minutes.

Throughout his various visits to Damascus, Hans remained the teacher in his relationship with Yune. Such was the case until June of 1999 when he arrived in Damascus on a three-day consultancy. Yune then was in the midst of trying to find a small piece of land in the Ghuta, the fields of walnut and apricot trees stretching around Damascus from Darya in the extreme west to Irbin in the extreme east. Yune became interested in the Ghuta after having read in a book that this area was in fact the wilderness of Damascus and that it had special significance at the ends of time. After office hours, he drove Hans to the plot of land he was most inclined to purchase near a small town named Dier al-Asafir, or the Monastery of Birds, around 22 km north east of Damascus. The land had an old wooden gate and inside, amid the walnut trees, there was a well and a small cabin where shovels and old bags were stored. They sat on the grass near a large walnut tree. Suddenly, it was Yune who was speaking with authority.

"So who's Kirsten?"

"You must have heard me speak on the phone. Kirsten is my girlfriend."

"I thought you were married?"

"Eva and I are separated."

Hans smiled as though trying to make sure that Yune really wanted to listen to the story he was eager to share. Yune smiled back in a manner that confirmed that he was very much interested in listening to anything Hans was willing to speak about.

"You see, Dr. Yune ..."

"Let's put aside our titles," Yune said as he touched Hans on the shoulder. Did Yune realize how much energy was radiating from his hand to Hans?

"It's really very complicated. I don't mean just my story but everything happening in Germany and in the west."

"What is complicated?"

"Relationships and everything that has to do with intimacy! I'm separated from Eva because she had an affair with Josef, my son's piano teacher. But she doesn't know that I was having an affair with Kirsten long before Josef became my son's piano instructor. Kirsten is divorced, and has two children. She was divorced when I met her, but she still lives with her boyfriend and his two children. So, you can say she's cheating on her boyfriend with me!"

Hans was speaking as though racing to expunge himself from a dark weight that had long sat on his heart.

"It's like the institution of marriage in the entire Western world has been placed under a curse that is so powerful that no one, no one Yune is protected from it!"

Hans now changed the way he was sitting and tilted his head toward Yune.

"I'm so tired of all this cheating. But the curse follows us everywhere. I cannot remember one relationship that began in purity and remained pure! I just want to start all over again. There's this beautiful cathedral in Cologne. My mother would take me there when I was young. I loved to go because I was fascinated by the Shrine of the Three Kings. You must have heard of the Three Kings? They were Persian. How fascinating! I often put myself to sleep fantasizing about being one of them. I see myself following the star of Bethlehem until it leads me to Christ."

Yune smiled warmly.

"I walked into this cathedral one day. I still don't know why I did. I had deliberately avoided it for more than twenty years. My mother had always told me that I would go back, but I would just laugh and dismiss her. So I sit on one of the benches and minutes later, a woman walks in and sits down next to me. The entire cathedral is empty, but she sits down right next to me. I turn my head to her, and we start talking. Her name is Heidi and it suddenly becomes clear that she's everything I have ever wanted in a woman and in a wife. But Yune, I'm so scared."

"Of what?"

"Of the curse. Every time I try to start again, the curse strikes back. Any minute now, Kirsten is going to find out that I'm in love with Heidi. Any minute now she's going to ask me to get out of her life, as I once asked Eva to do. Yune, someone has to stop this! All I want is to start all over again, to love Heidi and be loved by her, and to be blessed in this love until the day I die."

Yune spoke with authority and intense emotional depth.

"Hans, I will take you and Heidi out of this curse if you promise to be among the twelve."

"What twelve?"

"The twelve who will be there when Christ will return to remove this entire earth from the curse of lust and the curse of hate."

Hans looked shocked, and despite his entire intellectual training which had taught him to doubt everything that cannot be objectively demonstrated, he could not dispute the authority with which Yune was speaking.

"I want you to be here in Damascus on the 24th of December this year."

"Christmas Eve?"

"Yes. Bring Heidi if you wish."

"And the curse?"

"The curse has already been removed. When you go back to Cologne you will find that everything has been prepared for an eternal and faithful bond with Heidi."

Hans, now fully realizing he was in contact with an authority of a type he never realized existed, rushed to squeeze in yet another request:

"And Alyson?"

"Alyson?"

"My daughter. I want her to be protected from the curse as well."

Yune closed his eyes.

"She is protected."

Hans reached to Yune's hand as though to thank him and confirm the covenant they had just made. Yune pressed his hand tightly.

"Christmas Eve?"

"Christmas Eve."

Majduleen Haddad

Majduleen, or Leen as she was called by everyone, was a married woman in her mid-thirties who had previously worked as an English instructor. Here at UNESCO, Leen was the epitome of the child living amongst the dark objects of this world. She worked a lot, spoke very little and expected nothing. She used her entire salary to support her family, keeping for herself only enough to buy her Pall Mall cigarettes and to occasionally help an old woman named Afifa who would wander the streets near her home.

Yune liked to spend time at Leen's office. It was a place where he felt he could hide from the various visitors he received on a daily basis. Rakan, his secretary, knew of course where he was but understood that his presence at Leen's office meant that he wasn't in a mood to see anyone. Until this point, Yune hadn't spoken much to Leen. He would sit in her office and read a newspaper or just have a cup of tea. But on this day, Yune entered Leen's office not to escape but rather to make yet another covenant.

"Leen, when was the last time you slept through the night?"

Leen, who was typing when Yune walked in her office, raised her head and stared at Yune in disbelief.

"What?"

"I asked when was the last time you slept through the night was. But I already know."

"What do you know?"

"I know how you lie on your bed and stare at the ceiling, how you stay awake like this until the call for prayer at dawn."

"Who told you this?"

"And I know how you spend all that time trying so hard to answer one question."

"What question?"

"I'll tell you the question, but will you trust my answer?"

Leen stared at Yune fully convinced that none of this could possibly be taking place. She reached for her pack of cigarettes, as though to seek some form of protection or perhaps inspiration.

"I don't know. I'm not sure I know what you are talking about. But yes, if you share with me the question, I will trust that you must know the answer."

"Is this all I was created for? You spend all night wondering, is this all I was created for?"

Yune said this and reached for Leen's hand.

Leen didn't resist. It was his hand over hers and her hand over the pack of cigarettes.

"What's the answer?"

"The answer is no."

"No?"

"No, Leen, you were not created just for this."

❖

The Gospel of Damascus

Majduleen Haddad was born in the northern Syrian city of Dier al-Zur. Aboud Haddad, her great grandfather, was born in 1895. In 1919, at the collapse of the Ottoman Empire, hundreds of Armenians escaped the violence in Anatolia and headed south towards Dier al-Zur. At the outskirts of Dier al-Zur, Aboud owned a piece of land in a village named Kisrah. Every Friday, his parents and younger brothers and sisters would gather there. But Aboud would go on Thursday afternoon to enjoy the place before it was filled with noise. It was on one of those Thursdays back in March 1919, that Aboud heard a voice, something resembling the sound of a child who had been crying for hours and whose crying had now become more of a deep moaning. He walked towards the fig tree, the oldest tree in his land. His eyes caught the image of a color, a golden red color not at all consistent with the colors Aboud had come to associate with his land. Lying behind the tree was a young teenage girl in a black long dress. Her golden-red hair was long and braided though the braids were clearly tied a few days ago. As he carried her all the way back to his home in Dier al-Zur, she was too frail and weak to be described as fully conscious.

That was the beginning of the story. Later he would learn that her name was Alexi and that she had witnessed the killing of her entire family. She doesn't know why she was spared. She had wandered for more than three days until Aboud found her in Kisrah near the old fig tree. Aboud had trouble pronouncing 'Alexi' so he called her Fida, Arabic for silver, because of her pale complexion. And in less than six months, Aboud and Fida were married. Her son Omar was Majduleen's grandfather. Fida remained Christian until her death and Aboud was careful, at least once a month, to take her to Aleppo so she could attend Sunday mass at the Forty Martyrs Armenian Cathedral. Later, a church would be built in Dier al-Zur commemorating the Armenians who died in the early twentieth-century, but that was after Fida had died.

✦

Ever since Yune's first serious talk with Leen, she became fully preoccupied with his visits to her office. She tried to make her office as pleasant as possible in his eyes. She connected her computer to a small set of speakers so Yune could listen to her favorite songs as he read his newspaper. She placed a crystal bowl on her glass coffee table and made sure it was always full of tangerines. She even bought an electric coffee maker so there was always a hot cup of coffee awaiting his arrival. And, in turn, Yune became entirely heedless of how the hours he spent in the office of a married woman were interpreted and spoken of by his colleagues. Often, he relied on his assistant, Rakan, to cover up for him, especially after he felt Rakan had become one of the twelve.

How did Yune spend his time there? He would walk in and reach for something to read. A cup of coffee would be poured. A tangerine might follow. And then Leen would begin to speak. To an analytic observer, it was clear that Leen had adopted Yune as her personal therapist and that she had done so on the basis of the strong spiritual trust which he had managed to instill within her. Yune would let her speak until he felt it was time to share something—something that would both comfort her but also reinforce her identity as one of the twelve. My favorite memory of their encounters was the day on which Yune managed to teach her both *zikr* and twirling in the span of an hour.

Though it was deeper and darker, Leen's hair was still reminiscent of her great-grandmother's. And her face still had hints of Fida's light freckles. On this particular day, she was wearing a long, white, cotton dress.

"I often think about what you said."

Yune remained focused on his newspaper. Leen lit a cigarette.

"You know how I don't sleep. I never shared that with anyone. My husband says it's healthy not to sleep. I should get out of bed and pray when I can't. He says that's what he would do, but he never asks me why I can't sleep."

She turned her head toward the window to her left and blew smoke in its direction.

"First it's the sound. Everything has a noise you know. I leave my bed and go searching for sources of sound. I start with the obvious, the clock on the wall, the faucet dripping, or even the refrigerator. Sometimes, I can hear the electricity traveling in the walls."

Yune put his newspaper down.

"So I just turn off the main switch. A few seconds follow of beautiful silence. But when I'm back in my bed I discover the sound that was haunting me from the very beginning. The sound of him next to me. What does one do when she discovers a sound that reminds her of all the times she was silenced? With every breath he exhales, I remember all the times when I felt I couldn't breathe.

And so my second journey begins. This time I want air. I go around the house opening windows. It doesn't matter what the weather is like. There's no oxygen inside the house. I lie down again. Now I can breathe, but the open windows bring in the sounds of cars and trucks. Sometimes I can even hear airplanes.

Close friends, family, they come to me. I don't know what they notice? Do they notice me or him? They say I should be patient though I don't speak about being impatient. But I wonder, could they go through life unable to sleep? Others say, it's my fault, because I never respond, I never draw lines, they say. I guess I could draw lines. But what would that be? People draw lines in companies. Supervisors draw lines with employees. But are you really supposed to draw lines with the very person you sleep with? Or should I say, can't fall asleep with?"

All this time, Yune's head was looking down. Now he finally turned to her.

"I know a way to stop all the sound."

Leen stood up and walked towards the window. She was standing right in front of him now and was focused entirely on what he was saying.

"It's called cave time."

"Cave time?"

"When you're in your bed, close your eyes, take a deep breath and repeat, not with your tongue, but with your heart."

"What do I repeat?"

"God is with me. Watching me. Witnessing me."

Leen repeated the words as Yune had said them, as though already rehearsing for her night time performance.

"Then you will start seeing the name of God engraved in white light on your heart. A moment will then come when you will enter cave time."

"What is cave time?"

"It's when your sense of sound, time and place just leave you."

"What happens then?"

"This you have to taste."

"What happens to you in cave time?"

"I see Christ suddenly arriving. Sometimes he arrives at night. Sometimes he arrives at noon. Sometimes it's very crowded. Sometimes, I'm the only one there."

Leen then reached for her mouse and pressed the play button.

"There's a song you just have to hear. I don't know why, but it always reminds me of things you say."

It was a song by the Beatles.

Words are flying out like
endless rain into a paper cup
They slither while they pass
They slip away across the universe
Pools of sorrow waves of joy
are drifting through my open mind
Possessing and caressing me

Yune stood up, moved the table toward the wall and, as Nouri once did in his presence, began to slowly twirl.

Jai guru deva om
Nothing's gonna change my world

He looked at Leen who was standing and watching in awe.

"Don't hesitate."

And Leen didn't.

Nothing's gonna change my world
Nothing's gonna change my world
Nothing's gonna change my world

It was as they were both twirling in Leen's small office that suddenly Rakan walked in. His face turned red. He wasn't pleased, but he said nothing.

Eleven

Yune failed to identify an eleventh disciple until a day arrived when a man walked in his office. His eyes were a shocking green that perfectly matched the color of his jacket.

"Have a seat please, may I help you?"

"I can't be long; I came to tell you to stop searching. I am eleven!"

"Eleven?"

"Yes, I am number eleven. I was chosen by the One you are waiting for. And I will be there with you when he arrives."

The man said these words and left, leaving Yune in tears.

❖❖❖

Omar Imady

VII. The Sign of Jonah

Omar Imady

1

"What do you mean it's not glowing?"

"It's just not glowing, Risha!"

"But Raqeem, it's the seventh cylinder, the last cylinder and the disciples have all been identified. They are ready to be there when "Damascus is remade." So, now we need to know when exactly this is supposed to take place."

"Well, Yune seems to think it's going to be on the 24th of December, 1999! He's going around and sharing this with the disciples and he even began to plan the event."

"What event?"

"The night when he believes Christ will return. He's come up with this elaborate interfaith celebration during which he's convinced an unexpected guest will arrive."

"But why 1999?"

"Perhaps he thinks it's the last year of the millennium."

"He's a year off you know. The last year of the millennium is 2000!"

"Maybe he's just tuned to an inner calendar."

"All this without instructions?"

"Nothing is glowing, Risha."

The Grand Mosque – Friday, December 24th 1999

During all the years Yune spent at UNESCO, there were two periods during which he felt blessed to be an employee of this organization. The first of course was when he began his search for disciples, and the second was when he realized that UNESCO was the ideal institution through which he could plan and execute an interfaith celebration at the Grand Mosque of Damascus. UNESCO is all about culture, and what could possibly surpass the cultural dimensions of such an event? The VIP list was long and impressive. It included the Minister of Culture, under whose patronage the event was going to take place, foreign ambassadors and the heads of all international organizations based in Damascus. A wooden stage was placed in the courtyard of the Grand Mosque and the Minaret of Christ was set to be flooded with light at exactly midnight. Yune got all this approved, but he wanted much more. Top on his list of requests was getting rid of the ugly electricity room attached to the outer southern wall, where a lintel still stood marking the now blocked central gate of the once Cathedral of John. He also wanted the Greek inscription on the lintel to be fully restored: "Thy kingdom, O Christ, is an everlasting kingdom, and Thy dominion endureth throughout all generations." Yune regarded the survival of this inscription as far more significant than Hans' infamous figs of Baal. Why all the zealots of the last fourteen centuries had failed to identify and obliterate it served only to confirm, in Yune's mind and heart, that this was indeed the landing site of Christ. But the electricity room stayed and the official from the Ministry of Culture with whom Yune was arranging the event warned him that insisting on such "nonsense" may risk the entire project.

There was one request which Yune kept secret from everyone. The Minaret of Christ had one door at its base which was connected by a passage to the courtyard of the mosque. It was almost always locked, especially since electricity, tape recorders, and microphones made it unnecessary for the *muazzins,* or those who called for prayer, to climb up the minarets of the mosque five times a day. Yune wanted this door left open, not because he thought a mere lock could present an obstacle to the entrance of Christ but because he felt it was more respectful to keep it open. A sign, as it were, confirming how welcome Christ was. And so Yune, asked Nabeel and Nabeel, without anyone noticing, ensured it was indeed left unlocked.

In his mind, Yune could visualize the entire event. He saw Christ first arriving on the terrace of the Minaret of Christ carried by angels as the prophet of Islam once prophesied. In most of his visions, he saw this happening late at night. Droplets of water, resembling beautiful pearls, would fall from his hair, confirming that he was indeed the Anointed One. He would then climb down the stairs and enter the mosque. Once inside, he would approach the Shrine of John. Yune could see him standing next to the Shrine with his eyes closed. Later, after performing the dawn prayer, he would exit the mosque with his followers. There was only one problem to his vision of the event. He saw Christ exit through the gate that had the Greek inscription engraved above it. A royal departure, as it were. But this gate, of course, had been blocked ever since it had become part of the southern wall of the mosque. And the mere mention of a wish to open it would render Yune clinically insane in the eyes of most Damascenes!

Representatives of every possible Christian denomination were invited to read their religious scriptures documenting the birth of Jesus in five liturgical languages. The birth of Christ would be recited from the New Testament in Arabic, Greek, Latin, Armenian, and Syriac. In addition, the birth of Christ was also to be read by two Muslim Qur'anic reciters, one reading verses from *The House of Amram* and, the other, verses from *Mary*. In all, seven reciters would be sitting on the stage, five Christians and two Muslims. Children dressed in white and carrying white roses would stand around the front, right and left sides of the stage. Around one hundred chairs were placed in the western part of the courtyard which guaranteed most guests a view of the upper part of the Minaret of Christ. For some reason, Yune decided that only sparkling ginger would be served, possibly inspired by a Qur'anic reference to a drink of ginger in paradise.

All twelve disciples, including Yune of course, managed to attend the event in different capacities. But only Risha and I, from among the eight were there, disguised as members of the diplomatic corps. My remaining six companions were right in pointing out that none of this was inspired by anything from Wahi and that in the absence of a cylinder glowing and a message that clearly points at what should be done, they simply would remain in their caves! They weren't the only ones to boycott the event. Of Yune's entire family, only his father agreed to come. Amanda felt all of this was nothing but a creative distraction that Yune had come up with to ignore his responsibilities to his family, and Maryam simply couldn't relate to the spiritual implications of the event.

Yune was dressed in a very elegant white suit. Everything about him on that night seemed to be spectacular. At least, that's how Risha kept referring to her child. Yune climbed the stage and as he adjusted the microphone, he seemed suddenly to pause. I wondered if he was recollecting the dream he once had of standing on a stage just like this one in the courtyard of the Grand Mosque. In the dream, he woke up just before he started to speak. But this wasn't a dream. After welcoming everyone to this event and noting the cooperation of UNESCO and the Ministry of Culture toward ensuring its success, Yune surprised everyone, by choosing to recite a segment from a poem he wrote shortly after Nouri died.

> *And so you have chosen to wait.*
> *So as to state that it's not too late*
> *to step aside.*
> *Let them carry the cross.*

Nail the smiles of innocence.
Pierce the breath of purity.
And distribute the garments of light.
Not you.
You close your eyes and dream of a day when –
When the eastern star will reappear.
Never having experienced death.
To restore to earth its forgotten spring.
To give us back our wedding ring.
And so you have chosen to wait.

Yune returned to his seat in the front row and the beautiful recitations began, timed to end moments before midnight. Risha looked so beautiful on this night. She was wearing a tiara with a row of green enameled flowers, a pine green velvet dress, and a pearl necklace. When the final recitation from *Mary* began, she seemed totally transfixed.

> *And mention in this Book the account of Mary when she withdrew from her people to an eastern place ... We sent unto her Our Spirit who appeared to her in the form of a perfect man.*

> *She said: I seek refuge in God, the Most Merciful, from you! ... He answered: I am but a messenger sent from your Lord, to give you a pure son.*

> *She said: How shall I have a son when no man has touched me, neither have I been unchaste?*

The recitation from Mary ended with the following words spoken by the infant Christ:

*And Peace be upon me, the day I was born,
and the day that I die, and the day I am raised
up alive.*

With these words, the recitations were over. I turned to
Risha and whispered: "I have a tense feeling." She seemed
surprised and didn't answer. When, a few minutes later,
midnight arrived and the Minaret glowed in light against
the night sky, everyone broke out in applause, everyone except for Yune and eleven others whose eyes were fixed at the
Minaret, waiting for something to take place that resembled,
however remotely, their image of the Second Coming of
Christ. But only the waiters carrying the trays of sparkling
ginger arrived. And as the drinks were being served, Risha
and I saw Yune quickly leaving the scene. Alisar also noticed and she quickly followed him as he exited the mosque
through the western gate.

Yune headed left, then right towards the Street That is
Straight. He ran for fifteen minutes until he reached the Roman Arch, right next to al-Maryamiyah or St. Mary's Church.
There a Roman arch stood. Attached to the arch was a small
white minaret. During his tours of Old Damascus, Yune had
noticed this minaret and felt that perhaps, just perhaps it
was the real Minaret of Christ. Yune arrived out of breath.
A few meters behind him stood Alisar, holding her shoes
in her hand. He looked up, and then around, as though trying to make sure he wasn't missing anything. Perhaps Christ
had already arrived? Perhaps he was standing near the pavement? Perhaps he was disappointed that no one was there
to greet him? Then Yune started to run again, He ran 700
meters towards Bab Sharqi or the Eastern Gate. This was the
last possible place. Another small white minaret erected over
the Eastern Gate. Yune examined the place again. And again
there was no one there but himself. Alisar called out from

behind him. "Yune, stop, please stop." She rushed towards him, took hold of his hand and led him away.

✢

Omar Imady

2

The immediate events that followed that night tell a story I don't like to recollect. A story of how the man my companions and I helped educate and prepare, broke and shattered like a crystal vase hitting the floor. Yune had traveled to the Minaret of Christ, as he had once traveled to Narvik, and had found no one there but himself, no voice to hear but his own.

To those of course who regarded the event as an interfaith celebration, it was a grand success. But to those who believed in Yune, the event was the most disappointing moment of their lives. And the days that followed carried more pain and disappointment. Much of the material used to vilify Yune was provided by Rakan, his assistant. Thus, Yune became a womanizer who danced in his office with married women and spent hours talking about his heretical views with foreigners! Yune was far too sensitive to deal with any of this and so his subsequent resignation from UNESCO was not a surprise. Yune was also accused of having ascribed to Nouri words he didn't say. Rakan had a copy of *The Gospel of Damascus* which Yune had shared with all the disciples, and he made it available to many of Nouri's acquaintances who sadly fell into the trap and accused Yune of falsifying Nouri's words. They were all aware of how close Yune was to Nouri in the last two years of his life, and that alone should have made them careful not to make such accusations. Only the disciples, not counting Rakan of course, didn't take part in any of this. They were disappointed, but their hearts remained loyal despite the conflicting noise in their heads.

When Nouri died, it took around three days for Yune to come back to normal activity. This time it took forty. When the forty days of mourning were over, Yune began to be responsible again, but joy and laughter seemed as though they had been totally extracted from his heart. From one of the highest positions in the UN in Syria, Yune became a teacher at a small international high school. He applied to the school in time to join in the spring semester. Many disciples, after having recovered from their initial disappointment, tried their best to comfort him. They tried also to determine if he could explain what had taken place. But Yune was in no state to provide anyone with an explanation. And whatever help that was proposed, he was adamant to push it away.

During the day, Yune was torn between two strong contradictory feelings. The first was that he was let down. At times, he even felt deceived, led to believe something remarkable. A vision that he would never have embraced had it not been for a series of events that he could trace as far back as Maryam's bedtime stories. Then there was the other feeling, the feeling that he must have been so arrogant, so hypnotized by an exaggerated sense of self importance, to believe in the whole idea of his role in the Second Coming and, worst of all, to act upon it.

During the night, Yune had to deal with a different feeling, a feeling that forced him to explore the boundaries of insomnia. Yune, who once taught others how to sleep, was now the one staring at the ceiling. This feeling was about longing. He missed Nouri and, even more, he missed Nouri's vision of the coming of Christ. He missed his faith in this vision; he missed the sweetness it carried for him, the optimism and the sense of purpose. He missed it all, and it's not easy to fall asleep when you're overwhelmed by longing.

The Gospel of Damascus

Throughout all of this, the seventh cylinder failed to glow. I often contemplated asking Wahi for an explanation. Once, I actually did send him a message. But he didn't answer, and I felt it was too impolite to persist. My companions and I returned to lesser tasks that didn't require golden scrolls, and none of us, with very infrequent exceptions by Risha, engaged in any discussion that had to do with Yune. I appreciated this silence because I understood that it was out of respect to me. My companions knew all too well the special status which Yune had acquired in my heart, and none of them wanted to say anything that would sound insensitive or patronizing.

❖

And the years passed. Much of what Nouri predicted would unfold in the world took place. The new Roman Empire, or the Union of Free Nations (UFN) as it came to be known, grew to an extent unprecedented in human history and all of its enemies were defeated. But I was more interested in what was taking place with Yune. What I did once out of a sense of duty, I now did simply because I missed him. How often would I sit and watch Yune projected on the wall of my cave. He had been broken, but in the form of fragments he had become far more humble. The almost arrogant confidence that came with his conviction that he was entrusted with an important task had all disappeared.

In time, a house was built over the land he had once purchased in the Ghuta, the Biblical wilderness of Damascus, and he began to spend his evenings there, mostly meditating and reflecting and walking around his garden. Yet, his dedication to his family and his willingness to perform husband and father duties actually increased. All the bitterness he once harbored toward Amanda also disappeared. For how could he possibly judge her for being overly consumed with pursuing a way of life that brought her peace when he allowed himself to be fully consumed with a vision that proved to be a figment of his imagination? In a sense, Yune had finally become a child, as he once wrote in his poems, not because he felt the idea was poetic, but rather because he truly was transported from the anticipated glory of that night to the "forgotten corners" of his Ghuta house.

There was, of course, one cylinder left and Risha and I had both independently reached the conclusion that it must contain a message inviting us to be there when Yune finally died, a farewell of some sorts. But why all of this had to take place, why we had to fulfill all of these Yune-related missions was a question none of us had an answer to. But angels are not human. We can come to terms with mysteries. Our innate humility eventually overtakes us. The very creation of Adam was a mystery to us, and the way in which most humans have behaved since has not served to help us understand the exact purpose of this creation.

✛

It was in early 2020 when a spiritual movement started to gain the attention of the media. It gained my attention a few months earlier because a representative of this movement arrived at Yune's Ghuta house one December evening, uninvited and completely unexpected.

"Hans. Hans Siebold. What brings you here?"

"Yune, my teacher, I have come to share with you something very important."

"Please, don't call me that. Come; have a seat, my friend, Tea perhaps?"

"Yes, tea would be wonderful."

"I won't take much of your time. You may remember that I can be very precise."

Yune smiled. He was somewhat scared of what this was all about. But he was so pleased to see a man who still held a very special place in his heart.

"I have come to tell you a story you are not aware of. After the event ..."

Hans said "event" as though not quite sure how to refer to that night back in December 1999 without upsetting Yune.

"We, I mean the eleven, well, actually, the ten of us .."

That was another point that Hans clearly wanted to avoid, the betrayal of Rakan. Yune placed a cup of green tea on a large round table near Hans.

"Thank you. So, we met, and we agreed that we would all go back to our countries and try to forget it all for forty days."

"I mourned for forty days," Yune whispered as though he was speaking to himself, and Hans felt it would be impolite to act as though he had heard him.

"And if by the end of these forty days, some of us or all of us had moved on, then we would never meet again, but if every one of us still felt as though we should meet, then we would. We chose Konya. I forget who proposed it. But we chose Konya as the place where we would all meet if, and only if, we all still couldn't forget the words you once shared with us. By the fortieth night, I was still as passionately convinced of the truth and light contained in *The Gospel of Damascus* as I ever was."

"And the rest?"

"Well, I didn't know. And I decided I wouldn't phone or ask. I would just travel to Konya. And I did. When I arrived there, I found that Alisar and Majduleen had been there for more than a week, and the rest had arrived the day before I did. It was then that we decided in the Shrine of Rumi to reaffirm our covenant. Yes, Christ had not arrived, but Nouri had said nothing about the exact date he would arrive. So that ceased to be an issue for us. We would return to our countries and spread Nouri's words."

Yune now looked as though he couldn't believe what he was hearing. As he was living his broken life, all of this was going on. While he remained in the Ghuta unable to go beyond his longing, the disciples were going around changing the world.

"And so we started. It was difficult at first. We would invite our closest friends and family members and just sit with them, meditate and then read excerpts from *The Gospel of Damascus*. The first year was the hardest. But then the numbers increased and increased. Until it became clear that we have become such a large movement spreading across four continents."

"How many are you?" Yune said expecting to hear something in the vicinity of a few hundred.

"No one really knows how many we are because Nouri didn't really teach us to look different. We still speak of ourselves as belonging to the religions we were born into. We don't dress differently. Because we emphasize transcendence and oneness, some Christians first thought of us as a new version of Unitarianism. But over the years we have become known as Nouris! I've heard we may have around seven million members and perhaps far more sympathizers."

"Seven million?"

"Yes. You can estimate this by entries into our websites and blogs. And by how many offers we get from advertising agencies. Of course, some of our visitors are hostile, but only some."

"I can't believe this, and why have you chosen to visit me tonight? Why not one of the Syrian disciples?"

"You see, we still meet at least once a year, always in Konya. We met a few days ago. We were only nine. Nabeel, as you may have heard, died recently."

"I didn't know." It was clearly very sad and somewhat awkward that Hans from Cologne would know about Nabeel dying in Damascus, and Yune wouldn't.

"It was very tragic for all of us. He truly loved you and believed in you to the very end. Anyway, he was the only one left in Syria. Alejandra is in Madrid, Eva and Alisar live in the US, Tariq and Raydana are in Amman, Majduleen is in England, Sofiya is in Canada and I'm still in Cologne of course."

"Why did they all leave?"

"I guess they wanted to spread this message or perhaps they had some family reasons. I'm not really sure. So, the nine voted that I would visit you and that I should share with you what's going on. You see one of us had a dream. It was Leen. She dreamt that we all embarked on this beautiful ark. But our Noah wasn't with us!"

Yune looked as though he was about to cry.

"So we all agreed that we should now engage you and that we should start introducing the larger movement to you. And so here I am."

Yune paused for a few seconds before responding.

"Hans, your visit has truly touched me. I'm not exaggerating if I say that it's the most pleasant experience I have had in twenty years, but I can't meet your brothers and sisters in faith because there is something in me that has not healed. I wouldn't want this to be felt by them. I wouldn't want to have a negative impact on them. Please, don't misunderstand what I am saying. I truly believe that this movement is willed and blessed by God. But still I'm not yet ready, maybe soon, maybe never." Hans didn't wait for Yune to finish his words. It wasn't a very German thing to do, but he stood up and rushed to Yune who was sitting opposite from him and hugged him for a few seconds. They both cried, as though finally releasing the sadness of the last twenty years.

✤

The Nouris were not feared by political authorities because they had no political agenda. They were law-abiding, and they wouldn't dream of hurting an animal, let alone an innocent human being. And they genuinely respected the freedoms and human rights which this extensive secular empire upheld, but they did not respect its materialism. In fact, in an age when church attendance had gone below 5% in the west, they represented the only dynamic spiritual force that not only resisted materialism but that was systematically attracting people away from it. One didn't have to convert to become a Nouri. Everyone kept their own religion, but they did make the Nouri covenant which entailed important changes in the way they understood their faith and lived their lives.

❖

In early 2029, the peace that the world had enjoyed for so long was suddenly fractured. An eastern bloc of the UFN declared its independence. Under the leadership of a dark, yet very charismatic man, the bloc expanded. There was constant talk of war, and the UFN was not sure how to react. It couldn't possibly imagine that after all these years anyone would not want to be part of it, let alone go to war against it. With the weapons available to both sides, a war would mean destruction of a nature humanity had never yet witnessed. And so the UFN chose appeasement, which, for a while at least, seemed to work.

As far as the Nouris were concerned, the crisis was experienced in terms of what it implied for their activities and movement. To those Nouris living under the eastern alliance, many of their freedoms were curtailed since their commitment to their faith was regarded as subversive. To the Nouris living in countries that were still part of the UFN, their capacity to travel east became very restricted.

The Gospel of Damascus

In October 2031, the threat of war returned. This time nothing seemed capable of stopping it. Everyone agreed that a war would take place; the only question was when. As the world prepared for war, Nouris increased their missionary activity. Economic breakdowns and several devastating earthquakes delivered important blows to the illusionary promise of materialism and thereby facilitated the spread of the Nouri message. When the eastern bloc finally made its move, in mid 2032, it wasn't in the form of a missile attack. It was rather in the form of a massive movement of civilian population, accompanied by an equally massive number of soldiers that was heading west. All of this was in response to a speech by the leader of this bloc in which he called for a cleansing of the world from the principles upheld by the UFN. The mass human movement was to head west and "emancipate" all the cities it encountered along the way. West, of course, eventually meant Damascus. The UFN had not expected this. It was prepared to respond with overwhelming force from every possible direction. But how do you attack a multimillion civilian march? By late 2032, the massive movement had not only grown in size, despite the UFN's extensive attempts to contain it, but it also had reached the eastern boundaries of the Syrian Desert. Overtaking Damascus now seemed just a matter of time.

✣

Omar Imady

3

The Grand Mosque – Saturday, April 9th 2033

Seven years before my companions and I were destined to be retrieved, something extraordinary took place. It was a Saturday morning, and I had just returned from a brief mission in the town of Nabik, around fifty miles north of Damascus. I was asked to save an old man who lived there before the eastern march arrived. When I entered my cave, I felt this strong need to check on a box that I had not touched in years. Even before I opened it, it was clear that something was glowing within it. I felt something tighten within me. Was Yune about to die? I couldn't break the cylinder alone. I carried it and walked into Risha's cave.

"Please, stand next to me."

"It's glowing. It's glowing. Open it."

"I didn't want to do this alone."

"You're not alone. Open it."

I applied the pressure on the midpoint of the cylinder and it broke in its usual smooth manner.

"What does it say? Read out loud."

And I did:

Bring Jonah out of the sea.
The sky will be opened, and the earth will receive its long awaited Key.
Risha, Nur, Rahma, Sakinah, Mizan, Asa, Sur and Raqeem.
April 9-10, 2033 - Midnight - dawn

"Listen, I need to leave. I want you to inform our companions. I also want you to pull all the disciples into being at the Grand Mosque at midnight. Flights from Europe should be fairly easy. I'm not sure about Africa and Asia. Listen, if you have to, you and the companions are authorized to carry them straight into Damascus from wherever they happen to be. I'll take care of Yune."

"Yes. Don't worry; I will take care of everything. But Raqeem, they're eleven, not nine."

"Rakan is no longer one of them, and Nabeel died recently."

"Yes, I know. But Nur was asked to replace the missing two. I wasn't supposed to share this with you, but now everything has suddenly changed."

"Whom were they replaced by?"

"She wouldn't say. I just thought this was done to keep the Nouris going. I had no idea the disciples would ever meet at the Grand Mosque again."

"Neither did I, Risha. Not once did I imagine this would take place. Listen, I need to make sure everything is in order at the Grand Mosque. An hour or so before midnight, I have to bring Yune."

"OK, don't worry, we will all be there."

We both stared at each other for a few seconds as though suddenly realizing that the sweetness of facilitating Yune-related messages had so unexpectedly returned.

Over the next ten hours, my companions raced around the globe pulling disciples, and when necessary, carrying them on trips they were unlikely to ever forget. I also pulled the cleaners at the Grand Mosque into the most thorough cleaning job they have undertaken of the Mosque's carpets and outer courtyard.

I was finally ready to leave old Damascus and arrive at Yune's house in the Ghuta when suddenly a black Mercedes with shaded windows stopped next to me. The window opened.

"May I give you a ride?"

It was Wahi.

"Are you upset?"

"Not at all," I responded as I climbed into the front seat.

"Where are we going?"

"To a house in the Ghuta."

I had so many questions I wanted to ask, and I wasn't sure where I should start. But Wahi interrupted my thoughts.

"You do understand that at times even you cannot be fully informed because that would have an impact on how you felt toward the event. Your sadness was important, and so too was your sense of disappointment. Yune's heart is unconsciously linked to yours. There is a strong emotional bond even if he is unaware of it. If you had been made aware of what was going to take place tonight, your sense of relief would have been transmitted to him."

I couldn't help but interrupt. "What would have been so wrong with Yune feeling some comfort?" I asked this as I realized that we had arrived at Yune's house and that Wahi had parked the car right outside of the large green gate.

"Because he was supposed to be broken. You cannot receive the Christ triumphantly. Yes, his arrival is triumphant, but those who are meant to welcome him had to undergo the experience of being broken. With Yune, he also had to undergo the experience of being constantly embraced by a form of dark alienation visible only to him. But as difficult as it was, it still wasn't an actual whale!"

"A whale?"

"Yes, remember – Yune is Jonah!"

That obvious connection had actually never occurred to me.

"For each day, Jonah spent inside the whale, Yune had to spend eleven years inside his sense of grief, despair and loneliness. When Christ was asked for a sign, he would answer: "No sign shall be given except the sign of Jonah." This was said from the Christ who had performed numerous signs, including the sign of Lazarus. But he wasn't speaking of an event that would take place in Jerusalem two thousand years ago; he was speaking of an event that would take place two thousand years later. Yune's thirty-three years of living as a broken man in the wilderness of Damascus and his departure tonight to be there at the Grand Mosque is the sign of Jonah Christ once spoke of."

"But why 2033?"

"Two thousand years ago, in fact a week from today, Christ was raised over a Jerusalem that failed to appreciate the gift of the Christ. When he arrives tomorrow it will mark the day he triumphantly entered Jerusalem. You do realize tomorrow is Palm Sunday?

"..."

"It's also, by the way Ashura', the 10th of Muharam, the very day Noah was saved from the flood, Abraham from Nimrod, and Moses from Pharaoh."

Embarrassed from my failure to make all these connections, I looked at my watch.

"It's 11:30."

"Yes, please go knock on the door and ask him to come with us."

"Should I explain?"

"No, just knock on the door and ask politely. He won't resist. He's been feeling anxious all day. He hasn't felt so much anticipation in ..."

"Thirty-three years?"

"Yes."

I knocked at the door. Yune opened so quickly it was almost like he was standing right next to the door.

"Would you please come with me?"

Yune stared at me for a few seconds. It was the first time we had actually met face to face. He was still handsome and remarkably young looking.

"Yes. I will bring my jacket. It looks like it's about to rain."

Yune sat in the back of the car. Wahi greeted him with a majestic smile and steered his car toward old Damascus. As we reached the road of the Citadel that led directly to the Grand Mosque, I watched Yune from my side mirror. He seemed as though he understood it all far more than I ever did.

And then we arrived. Wahi parked the car near the Western gate and gestured to us to follow him. He walked to the left until he reached the road parallel to the Mosque's southern wall, the road that leads to the Minaret of Christ. The rain was heavier now, but it didn't seem to bother any of us. I looked above and saw that the sky was full of clouds that had descended way below—a sight I was familiar with in Mount Hermon but not in Damascus.

Yune walked very close to me. I wondered if he already realized how close he was to my heart.

"I can hear my mother singing," he whispered to me.

"What is she singing?"

"My eyes have seen the glory of the coming of the Lord."

I smiled. He was right on track.

Then, suddenly, the three of us stopped and stared in awe. Where the electricity room once stood, there was nothing but rubble. The large stones that had blocked the gate for over fourteen centuries were reduced to dust. The Greek inscription on the lintel above the gate seemed as though it was inscribed again in gold. A white light was shining from within the Mosque, strong enough to make the area immediately outside of the gate visible. My seven companions and the disciples stood on both sides of the gate. None of them had entered; they were waiting for Yune to arrive. In addition to the nine, Maryam and Amanda stood next to Nur in their sky blue coats, holding hands and smiling as though they had always believed they would be here. Some were blushing. Some seemed too dazed to express how they felt. Others were beaming with joy. Risha and Majduleen were twirling. Alisar was crying. Both Hans and Tariq approached Yune and patted him on the shoulder. Mizan was standing nearest to the entrance. He looked at Yune and said with his royal voice: "He arrived. He's climbed down the steps of the minaret, and he's now inside the mosque walking toward the Shrine of John." Wahi took Yune by the hand and led him inside into the light.

✣

During the seven years that followed, Christ and his followers, of whom the Nouris constituted the vast majority, defeated the soldiers of death and the apocalypse and, later, tore down the idols of materialism. By the time my companions and I were ready to be retrieved, earth had been spiritually revolutionized. But this is not the story I was asked to share. Mine is the story of the fire horse. A fire horse once carried Elijah to the sky. But when Christ returned, there was a fire horse waiting to greet him.

✣✣✣

The Epistle of Eliezer

Omar Imady

The Epistle of Eliezer

*Being a sacred history of Damascus compiled by Rabbi
Eliezer & sent to Rabbi Isaac of Aleppo*

While Damascus is clearly not the Jerusalem of the Judeo-Christian tradition or the Makkah of the Islamic tradition, it is nevertheless consistently invoked in Jewish, Christian and Islamic sacred literature. So surprisingly significant
are the language and contexts of some of these references
that the spiritual supremacy of the holy cities of Judaism,
Christianity and Islam appears to be challenged, thereby
tempting many classical commentators to either marginal-
ize such references or dismiss them as merely metaphori-
cal. Perhaps most significant are the references that involve
ascribing to Damascus a distinctive role in Jewish, Christian
and Islamic eschatology, namely, that of the landing site of
the Messiah or the Christ. Indeed, as the city of Christ, Damascus, not Jerusalem nor Makkah, embodies the promise
of spiritual renewal at the end of time. As such, the sacred
history of Damascus constitutes a significant linkage, as of
yet inadequately emphasized or documented, between the
three great monotheistic religions.

In *The Lives of the Saints*, more commonly known as *The
Golden Legend*, a collection of sacred traditions compiled by
Jacobus de Voragine, we read that Adam, and in turn all of his
descendants, are linked to Damascus in a very organic way:
" ... man was made in the field of Damascus." Not only does
Damascus provide the earth from which the first human was
made, but it is also the landing site of the first human community. "And so Adam was cast out of Paradise, and set in

the field of Damascus where as he was made and taken from, for to work and labour there."

Damascus is the place where Cane killed Abel. In the *Haggadah,* or the collection of lore and legends found in the Talmud, we read: "... the family of Cain resided in the field of Damascus, the spot whereon Abel was slain by Cain." In *Kunz al-'Ummal,* a large collection of Islamic Prophetic traditions, with varying degrees of authenticity, we also read: "I wish I was at this very moment in the wilderness of Damascus that I may visit the site where Prophets beseech the help of God, the site where the son of Adam killed his brother."

Sources do not link Damascus with Noah or the Flood. There is, however, a work ascribed to Shem, Noah's son and one of the seven Patriarchs of the world, which includes references to Damascus. *The Treatise of Shem* is an astrological almanac known from a 15th-century Syriac manuscript. It is apparently the only source in the category of the pseudepigrapha of the Hebrew Bible that contains references to Damascus: "And robbers will be gathered in Hauran and in Damascus ..." and "... there will be a disease in Damascus and in Hauran." These references, however, are clearly apocalyptic and do not shed light on the relationship, if any, between Shem and Damascus.

Nor is Eber, the great grandson of Shem, linked directly to Damascus in sacred texts. However, the Southern wall of the Grand Mosque of Damascus has a plaque that states, "This is the Spiritual Station of Eber." Some Muslim historians assert that Eber is buried under the wall at that very spot and that Damascus was actually built by Eber, the Hud of the Qur'an.

Interesting links between Abraham and Damascus are found in several sources. Abraham's trusted servant, Eliezer, is described in Genesis as "Eliezer of Damascus." Prior to the birth of Ishmael and Isaac, it was Eliezer who was destined to be the heir of Abraham.

How Eliezer came to be Abraham's servant is unclear. One would assume he was acquired by Abraham during his stay, or reign, in Damascus. Genesis, on the other hand, appears to imply that he was born in Abraham's house. The explanation advanced by the *Haggadah*, however, is that Eliezer, along with Ogi, or Og the king of Bashan, as he is more commonly referred to, were the gifts of Nimrod, a Mesopotamian monarch, to Abraham after Abraham's miraculous escape from the fire. As such, he is also credited with warning Abraham of Nimrod's plot to turn against him. Abraham's subsequent departure from Ur was based on Eliezer's warning. Alternatively, Eliezer is described as the actual son of Nimrod who abandons his father after watching Abraham's miraculous escape. Og, on the other hand, was one of the last of the giants; the only one from the Rephaim, the generation of the flood, to have survived; and the last of the offspring of the fallen angels and the daughters of Cain. He lived for centuries until he was killed by Moses near Edrei during the children of Israel's advance to the Promised Land.

Not only was Eliezer among the 318, born in Abraham's house, who fought along with Abraham against the kings who had taken Lot captive, but he was also the only one who was with Abraham during that wondrous event. The anomaly is resolved through revealing the numerical value of the letters in Eliezer's name (1 + 30 + 10 + 70 + 7 + 200 = 318). Another account further elaborates on the event. "Shem said to Eliezer: When the kings of the east and the west attacked you, what did you do? Eliezer replied: The Holy One, blessed be He, took Abraham and placed him at His right hand, and they threw dust which turned to swords, and chaff which turned to arrows ..." The fact that Eliezer is given the privilege of communicating with Shem is clearly indicative of his high spiritual status.

Eliezer was at times sent by Sarah, Abraham's wife, to enquire about Lot's wellbeing. To do so, Eliezer had to visit the infamous city of Sodom, the land of exotic justice and habits. Eliezer was both wise and witty, qualities amply confirmed by his encounters with the Sodomites. When Eliezer is asked to pay the man who had injured him, under the pretext that he was actually medically bled by him, Eliezer responds by throwing a stone at the judge and stating, "Pay my debt to the man and give me the balance." When asked to lie on the bed which is used to either stretch the body of a stranger, if he is found too short, or cut off his limbs, if he is found too tall, Eliezer responds by stating that at the death of his mother he had vowed never to sleep in a bed.

Other accounts also confer upon Eliezer a unique status given to only nine people. "Nine have entered alive into paradise, and these are:—Enoch, the son of Jared; Elijah; the Messiah; Eliezer, the servant of Abraham; Hiram, king of Tyre; Ebed Melech, the Ethiopian; Jabez, the son of Rabbi Yehuda the prince; Bathia, the daughter of Pharaoh; and Sarah, the daughter of Asher ..."

Eliezer is one of the very few Gentiles portrayed by Genesis and Genesis-related sources to have had such high spiritual qualities. Among other Gentiles, none seem to have risen to his status. Who else, after all, is known to have resembled Abraham spiritually and physically, as sources confirm? The fact that Eliezer was from Damascus serves to further bolster the distinct spiritual character of this ancient city.

Later, we find Damascus linked to David, through war and conquest, and to Solomon, through poetry. " ... thy nose is as the tower of Lebanon which looketh toward Damascus."

In the period immediately after Solomon, this history is taken over by the figures of Elijah and Elisha. Elisha is a Biblical and Qur'anic prophet, known in the Qur'an as al-Yasa'. Elisha was the man selected by God to become the prophetic heir of Elijah. Indeed, of the three major tasks which Elijah was asked to perform—anointing Hazael as king of Damascus, anointing Jehu as king of Israel and selecting Elisha as his disciple and successor—Elijah only performs the last. Perhaps he was too involved in a passionate battle with Ahab whose Phoenician wife Jezebel was seeking to introduce the cult of Baal into Israel, or perhaps Elijah regarded the anointing of Hazael and Jehu as tasks that he should delegate to his successor.

After Elijah's departure to heaven in a chariot of fire, Elisha takes on the Prophetic responsibilities, two of which will be directly related to Damascus. The first involves the figure of Naaman, an important Damascene general who was close to Ben-hadad II, the king of Syria. Naaman was highly respected for the victories he had helped secure for his people. Some sources credit him with having been responsible for the death of Ahab in the battle of Ramoth-gilead. But he suffered from leprosy and when he was told by his wife that their Jewish slave-maid claims that a man by the name of Elisha can cure him, he decided to pursue this possibility. Carrying a letter from his king, Naaman first visits the king of Israel, most probably Jehoram, son of Ahab, who is highly suspicious of the entire affair. But Elisha sends word to Naaman to bathe himself seven times in the Jordan River. At first, Naaman feels insulted. "Are not Abana and Pharpar, rivers of Damascus, better than all the waters of Israel? May I not wash in them, and be clean? So he turned and went away in a rage." But one of his attendants, however, advises him to test the Prophet's words and bathe himself in the Jordan. Naaman heeds the advice and is immediately cured. He visits Elisha not only to express his gratitude but also to proclaim his faith in Elisha's God. He further seeks to carry with him enough of Canaan's soil to erect an altar to Yahweh. Naaman only asks that he is pardoned for what appears to be part of his regular official duties. "When my master goeth into the house of Rimmon to worship there, and he leaneth on my hand, and I prostrate myself in the house of Rimmon, when I prostrate myself in the house of Rimmon, the Lord pardon thy servant in this thing." Elisha is understanding and responds by stating. "Go in peace ..."

In Naaman we have a Damascene figure reminiscent of Eliezer. He is respected not only by his people, but even by the Jewish slave-maid who appears genuinely to desire that her master is cured. "Would that my lord were with the prophet that is in Samaria! Then would he recover him of his leprosy." This must reflect the fact the she was well treated in this household. But most importantly, Naaman appears to have been divinely selected even before his encounter with Elisha. Indeed, of all the Syrian soldiers fighting against the army of Ahab, it is the arrow of Naaman, at the time only a common soldier, that is permitted to penetrate the armor of Ahab. As Jesus would later point out as he sought to discredit Jewish exclusiveness, there were many lepers at the time of Elisha, but God selected Naaman the Syrian as the only one worthy of being cured by Elisha. And there were many who had witnessed the miraculous acts of Elisha, including his close, yet disloyal, disciple Gehazi. But Naaman was among the few who responded in gratitude and faith.

"The wilderness of Damascus" is a term that is destined to take on highly significant eschatological associations, especially in Islam where it is the site of the Armageddon or the final battle between the forces of light and the forces of darkness. In 1 Kings, we read. "And the Lord said unto him: Go, return on thy way to the wilderness of Damascus;... and Elisha the son of Shaphat of Abelmeholah shalt thou anoint to be prophet in thy room." The idea of a divinely inspired entry into Damascus will be invoked centuries later by the Qumran community, using a verse in Amos as their Biblical foundation. "Therefore will I cause you to go into captivity beyond Damascus, saith the Lord." Indeed, to the Qumran community, the "new covenant" was made in the "Lands of Damascus." Furthermore, to the Qumran community, one of the attributes of their spiritual leader is the fact that he will enter Damascus. "The star is the Interpreter of the Law who shall come to Damascus; as it is written, A star shall come forth out of Jacob and a sceptre shall rise out of Israel." Later, the divine command is repeated to Paul. "Arise, and go into Damascus." Even Christ, in the Gospel of Barnabas—a medieval forgery but very likely based on a now lost original—travels to Damascus. "The day following there came, two by two, thirty-six of Jesus' disciples; and he abode in Damascus awaiting the other. And they mourned every one, for that they knew that Jesus must depart from the world." But it is perhaps the *Epistula Apostolorum*, or *Letter of the Apostles*, that makes the most profound proclamation. "Behold, out of Syria will I begin to call together a new Jerusalem."

Both Amos and Isaiah proclaim prophesies against Damascus. So, too, does Jeremiah, almost two centuries later. But in the midst of Jeremiah's prophecy against Damascus, we suddenly read. "How was the city of praise not fortified, the city of my joy?" This verse has constituted a dilemma for Biblical scholars. What possible significance does Damascus have that it may be described by God Himself as "the city of my joy" in this verse? Rashi attempts to solve the problem by ascribing the voice to the king of Damascus. Yet, both the previous and subsequent verses cannot be reconciled with such an interpretation. Others ascribe the verse to Jeremiah who is said to have had joyful days in Damascus. But all of this appears forced and de-contextualized. Further complicating such interpretations is the notion of "praise" associated with God, not idols. Thus, some scholars, though only a few, have ventured into interpreting this verse as spoken by God Himself. The verse would thus imply that Damascus, like Jerusalem, is being punished despite the fact that it is a city within which some do praise God and despite the fact that for reasons as of yet not revealed, Damascus is the city of God's joy.

Prophesying in the early Persian period, Zechariah differs from Amos, Isaiah and Jeremiah in that he does not appear to prophesy an imminent destruction of Damascus. Nevertheless, something is being prophesied and whatever it may be, it clearly relates to Damascus. It all really depends on how one translates, and in turn interprets, the fascinating 9:1 verse: "and Damascus shall be the rest thereof: when the eyes of man, as of all the tribes of Israel, shall be toward the Lord." Or: "And Damascus is His resting place, for man's eye shall be to the Lord and all the tribes of Israel." The confusion of this verse is evident in the following *midrash*. "Judah, our master, how long will you pervert the verses for us? I call heaven and earth to testify for me, that I am from Damascus, and there is a place named Hadrach. Now how do I explain: *And Damascus is His resting place*? [Rabbi Judah responded] That Jerusalem is destined to reach as far as Damascus. *His resting place* means only Jerusalem, as it is said: *This is My resting place to eternity.*"

But if verses and traditions in Judeo-Christian sacred literature that emphasize the status of Damascus in the ends of time can be misinterpreted, albeit with difficulty, their Islamic parallels are far more categorical. The Grand Mosque of Damascus has three towers or minarets. The eastern white minaret is known as the Minaret of Christ because Muslims believe it is the landing site of Christ in the ends of time. The foundation of this belief is a prophetic tradition that endows on Damascus a status which no other sacred tradition endows with this clarity:

"Jesus, the son of Mary, will descend on the White Tower, east of Damascus. He will be carried by two angels, his hands holding on to their wings. When he raises his head, droplets of water will fall like scattered pearls."

❖❖❖

Omar Imady

Disclaimer

This work is neither an autobiography nor a study in theology. It is a work of fiction – a novel.

Yes, it is at times inspired by real people and events that crossed my path. Yet, the attempt to derive an accurate representation of reality from such details will consistently lead to very strange and inaccurate conclusions.

It is also inspired by the breathtaking way God appears to intervene in our lives. But the attempt to derive theological conclusions from this novel about angels and their qualities and how the Divine Will is communicated to earth is again very likely to lead to conclusions never intended by the author.

I have done my best to show genuine respect to the traditions of all faiths. To those who may regard anything articulated in this novel, whether clearly expressed or simply implied, as offensive, I ask for your forgiveness and understanding.

Omar Imady

Other Books by MSI Press

Achieving Native-Like Second-Language Proficiency: Speaking

Achieving Native-Like Second-Language Proficiency: Writing

A Believer-in-Waiting's First Encounter with God

Blest Atheist

Communicate Focus: Teaching Foreign Language on the Basis of the Native Speaker's Communicative Focus

Diagnostic Assessment at the Distinguished-Superior Threshold

El Poder de lo Transpersonal

Forget the Goal: The Journey Counts...71 Jobs Later

How to Improve Your Foreign Language Proficiency Immediately

Individualized Study Plans for Very Advanced Students of Foreign Language

Losing My Voice and Finding Another

Mommy Poisoned Our House Guest

Puertas a la Eternidad

Road to Damascus

Syrian Folktales

Teaching and Learning to Near-Native Levels of Language Proficiency (Vol. 1-4)

Omar Imady

Teaching the Whole Class

The Rise and Fall of Muslim Civil Society

Thoughts without a Title

Understanding the People Around You: An Introduction to Socionics

What Works: Helping Students Reach Native-like Second-Language Competence

When You're Shoved from the Right, Look to the Left: Metaphors of Islamic Humanism

Working with Advanced Foreign Language Students

Journal for Distinguished Language Studies (annual issue)

The Gospel of Damascus

Omar Imady